JAMES D. JACKSON

SILK SHEETS

REGAL PAPERBACK FICTION
PUBLISHED BY REGAL PUBLISHING, INC.
UNITED STATES OF AMERICA

Copyright © 2002 by James D. Jackson

Regal Publishing, Inc., 2 Burbank Blvd, Savannah, Georgia 31419

Visit our Web site at http://www.regalpublishing.com

Printed in the United States of America

Library of Congress Cataloging-in-publication Data is available.

ISBN 0-9717355-1-4

PRAISE FOR JAMES D. JACKSON'S BOOKS:

"James Jackson hits the scene with a new voice, a thunderous tone and a lighting quick wit. This is a novel you will want to read again and again and again..." -*Timmothy B. McCann, National Best Selling Author of three novels: Until, Always, and Forever.*

"James Jackson is a wonderful storyteller. Silk Sheets is merely a testament to his magnificent storytelling ability."
- Joi Williams, CEO
Sankofa Counseling Center

"Very entertaining and riveting stories."
- The Birmingham Times

"Wrong Perception is more than a success story."
- Chicago Post Tribune

"Brief encounters of hot and heavy passion will grip you from beginning to end. Once you begin to read his books, you can't put them down." *- Washington Afro-American newspaper*

"Dr. Jackson masterfully explores love, compassion, and heartbreak. His characters live and breathe-they're funny and lovable, and true to life; his female characters give meaning to strength and courage." *- Michigan Chronicle*

ACKNOWLEDGEMENTS

Love knows no boundaries. This book honors extraordinary individuals who have found love irrespective of sexual orientation. To the awe-inspiring individuals who have shared insightful information, I express my gratitude.

I'm grateful for the love and support of my family and wonderful friends. I'd like to thank the entire Regal Publishing staff. To President, Comia Flynn, Vice President, Joi Williams, and National Marketing Director, Derrick Winston, thanks for believing in me and for your assistance in creating this novel. Also, I am deeply touched by the support of my editor Katrina Bateman, and the exchange of thoughts and stories we share.

I especially would like to thank my wife Sherrie for her ideas and above all, patience, my daughters, Jamie and Jessica, for their caring spirit, sense of humor, and unconditional love, best selling author, Timmothy McCann for his vote of confidence, and my best friend, Keith "Preacher" Brown, for his positive attitude towards life.

CHAPTER 1

Not long ago, I found myself sitting in the teachers lounge following an after school party. There were two teachers in the lounge, Mrs. Johnson and Mrs. Walker. They were in their early thirties, wearing power suits and slightly scuffed pumps. Mrs. Walker had a pleasant disposition, calm and soft-spoken most of the time.

I had daydreamed of clear, cloudless skies, cool, crisp air, and lazy mornings spent with a cup of hot chocolate and a good book. Boy was I looking forward to a relaxing summer vacation.

As I sat there completing my homework assignments, prior to heading home, I can still remember Mrs. Johnson, with a stern look on her face say, "Tanya Brown, please be careful walking home, okay?"

She knew my neighborhood, the people, and the ill-fated reality. I was being careful alright, but nothing could have prepared me for what ensued.

It was approximately 10:30 p.m. when several gunshots rang out. I hit the ground, scared and frazzled. Great, what now? I speculated. Then, as though my statement had been visionary, I heard gunshots again. Two shots were milliseconds apart, three more several seconds later. The first two shots caused me to freeze the following three galvanized me. I could hear the sounds of birds deserting a nearby tree. I noticed a black 4-door Mercedes in front of me; I could vaguely make out the silhouette of three husky men standing around the car, pistols drawn. After several more shots, the three of them jumped in the car and sped off. It looked like the E320, but I'm not certain. Hell, I'm not sure if it was even a Mercedes. It looked like a luxury car I do know that for sure.

Anyway, I heard stifled words and people screaming, but I couldn't make out whether they were saying that someone was dead or that someone got shot. Moment's later, eardrum-splitting screams congested the airway. I couldn't see much of anything it was unpleasantly murky that night. And although the moon was out, it wasn't shining down on me. I was near the sidewalk; face down, next to an enormously bulky tree.

The streetlights were inoperable and dogs began yelping their heads off. I turned my head slowly to the left to spit out the dirt and gravel that was wedged between my lips. *"Here we go again!"* I said in a faint whisper.

It wasn't bizarre for this to be transpiring shots rang out almost weekly in my locale. A*nother poor son-of-a-bitch* *probably dying from bullet wounds*, I considered. Last weekend the same thing. My next-door neighbor, Marcus Paige, was gunned down. I was at home, by myself, when the clamor began. I heard the sound of car tires coming to a screeching halt. Then a car door slammed. Marcus was apparently sitting on his porch when an unidentified assailant yelled, "You'll never fuck my wife again motherfucker!" The estranged man emptied the bullets from his 9mm into Marcus' neck, face, and chest. I counted five shots, but don't hold me to that either. When the car sped off, I looked out the window. Everything seemed tranquil, so I stepped outside. There I found Marcus in his wife's arms, with blood spewing out of his neck and mouth. I heard Lorraine, Marcus' wife, screaming at the top of her lungs, "Somebody, help me!" I ran back into the house, dialed 911. When I got back to Lorraine, I noticed that Marcus wasn't moving a muscle. We must have sat there twenty minutes or so before an ambulance arrived. When the ambulance did finally arrive, I watched the EMT personnel shaking their heads as to say, he was dead alright, dead as Benjamin Franklin. Marcus was a nice, hard-working man. I can say that about him. Just couldn't keep his dick in his pants.

On this night however, the story was much different. Frustrated and supremely irked, I dusted myself off and continued my walk home. I passed an alley where prostitutes normally earned their pay. That night was no exception. A voluptuous black woman was on her knees and a bald-headed potbelly white man, stood with his back to the wall smoking a cigarette. He was wearing gray slacks and a white button-down shirt. It was too dark to make out his shoes. They were dark colored shoes, but I'm not sure whether they were black or dark brown. The prostitute, however, had on a colorful outfit and she was a sexy, full figured, caramel-colored beauty. Why she hadn't married a wealthy man and preserved her dignity was beyond me. She was wearing her typical prostitute accouterments: Bob wig, nylon lavender blouse, black mini-skirt, fish net stocking, and black knee-high boots.

"Why don't you get a room?" I yelled.

That beautiful, yet, disgraceful whore, showed me the middle finger of her right hand, and without missing a beat, continued her head-bobbing rhythmic performance. "Go on home little girl. Mind your own damn business," the spineless jerk felt the need to bark in my direction. I stood there, briefly, just taking it all in. He exhaled a puff of smoke and shouted, "I'll pay you, just do it right!" I grimaced and walked on.

As I continued my journey, I stopped again and looked around at the neighborhood. I was appalled at what I saw. Stop signs riddled with bullet holes, dumpsters running over with maggots, and streets that had big potholes every ten feet or so.

So much impropriety happened here. Recalcitrant males shot out the streetlights to avoid being seen committing crimes at night. The glass from those same streetlights was scattered all over the street. Graffiti with the words "Fuck the Police" was spray painted on some of the walls. The police must have feared these imbeciles because they never stepped foot in the neighborhood.

Calling the Sheriff to come and clean up the place was like asking Monica Lewinski to swallow and keep her damn mouth shut. It wasn't happening now and it probably never would.

In the vacant homes, all of the windows were boarded up and the grass was at least three feet high. Beer bottles, paper bags, and soda cans found a home there. I watched prostitutes, drunks, and drug addicts find their way through the narrow cracks in the back door of some of these homes to handle their business. In the places where lights existed, I observed men begging for sex and prostitutes asking for money. What a piteous sight.

When I finally made it to my less than humble abode, I could only shake my head at the piss-poor place I called home. "Why?" I asked again, frowning to myself as I looked up at my old-dilapidated house. I should have slapped my mother and shot my father for asking me to move here. With two black shutters missing from my bedroom window and a front door that barely closed and needed painting, reaffirmed the obvious, we were poor as hell.

My house was the last house on the block. If you were facing my house, to the right was Lorraine's house and to the left was about six acres of woods.

Just as I was about to walk up the steps to my house, I was startled by what I thought was a sound coming from the woods. I turned and glanced in that direction, but I didn't see a thing. A few seconds later, I heard a female's voice. I tiptoed over to the woods to see what was going on. Surprisingly, it was my neighbor Charlene and her boyfriend Steven, getting it on. I stopped dead in my tracks and smiled. Charlene often bragged about how sexy he was, so I stuck my neck out as far as I could in hopes of watching. A full moon lit up the sky in more ways than one. As he elevated and descended, Charlene was laying on her back, perfectly still. I couldn't help laughing to myself as Steven performed his less-than-skillful act. He looked like he was having muscle spasms. When Steven asked, "Am I hurting you?" and Charlene stared blankly at him and replied, "No baby, I'm barely feeling anything." I was in stitches.

"Hey ya'll. I guess I caught you with your pants down, huh?" I said, as I stood up above the bush in plain view of them, cackling like a hyena.

Charlene cursed lavishly, "Get out of here girl, don't you have any respect?" Charlene asked.

"Oh, don't trip, you caught me with Tyrone and laughed all the way to the damn bank. Pay back is a bitch ain't it?"

"Go to hell Tanya!" Steven yelled, as he drew his hand back as if he was going to slap me. "Come on Charlene, let's get out of here," Steven implored while pulling up his pants to cover that little wee-wee of his.

Charlene got up, grabbed her clothes, and headed butt naked through the woods. For some reason, I found myself feeling sexually aroused when I gazed at Charlene's body. As her well-defined legs elevated her toned body, her beautifully colored high-yellow ass was screaming perfection. Booty so shapely and tight, you could bounce a quarter off it. She barely spoke to me before this episode, and it would be a while before she spoke to me again.

Seeing Charlene and Steven in the woods, however, was one of the better memories. Those woods, what memories I have. I can remember beautiful deer and white rabbits dashing or hopping their way through. Horrifically speaking, mangy dogs, rats, and dead humans were spotted there too, but I'd rather forget those reflections.

Some of my other neighborhood friends and I enjoyed playing hide and seek there. We also hid from our parents, kissed boys, and like Charlene, did the nasty there a time or two.

As I made my way out of the woods and started up the stairs leading to my front door, Kim Taylor was right behind me. Kim was a crackhead. In high school, she was the homecoming queen. A bad break-up with the love of her life sent her fairy tale existence into a pool of sexually transmitted diseases and drug addiction.

"Hey Tanya, you got a couple of dollars?" she asked.

I flinched and then said, "You scared the shit out of me." After a brief pause I remarked, "I don't have any money."

"Aw, come on girl, I'll do anything you want for a couple of dollars," she said as both hands went flying in the air like a preacher when he gestures for everyone in the congregation to stand.

"If I had it, I would give it to you. Go on home now Kim," I told her as I gave her the run-a-long gesture.

"Aw ight then," she said as she made her way up the road and out of sight.

My mother and father had me when they were in their teens. I'm told that my dad was so high on marijuana that he didn't remember having sex with my mother when I was conceived. He put up a big stink about it and everything. I was told by my mother that a paternity test had-to-be-done before my father agreed to have anything to do with me. At that time, my mother thought it best that my grandmother raise me. Off I went. *Wise choice mom.*

Now after thirteen years and a rocky marriage, my parents assured me that it was time to come home. My grandmother was getting older and not able to get around like she used to. Establishing rapport with my parents now was not only the right thing to do, I felt as though it was the only thing to do.

Before traveling north, however, I had been a virgin, optimistic, free-spirited. Not anymore. I caved in to the first and second boy that enchanted me within the first three weeks of my arrival. Both boys convinced me that they cared about me. Hell, Tyrone told me that he loved me to later dump me like a bad habit. My grandma forewarned me about the fast-talking boys up north. I guess I didn't pay much attention. Or better yet, I didn't want to. Those boys were fairly attractive and smooth talkers. Besides, my hormones were raging and I was a gullible, fourteen-year-old southern girl. Oh well.

After reflecting on a few of the wonderful memories, the ridiculous reality ensued. As I mentioned earlier, I had just returned home from an after school party held in my high school's gymnasium. The gym had very little ventilation and we were packed in there like sardines. Loud music, stank breath, and musty body odor filled the air. I was dank from perspiring most of the night, tired as hell from dancing, and, of course, the stroll home was no walk in the park.

Thank God for being poor and walking home nowadays though, the fat had vanished from my midsection and I was actually starting to see some definition in my legs. The only thing fat on me was my booty, or so I was told by the guys at school.

After making my way to the top of the steps, I realized that my black rayon shirt and tight navy blue Gloria Vanderbilt jeans were drenched with sweat. I wiped my brow before sitting down in my father's black rocking chair.

His chair was meticulously placed on the right side of our bay window so that he could see the dazzling park off in the distance. The brown swing was on the opposite side of the bay window but you really didn't have a good view of the park from there. Our porch was gray like our steps and it too could use a paint job and some repair.

During the summer, in the daytime, the park was engrossed with family's enjoying the walking track and the playground. The playground had a small amusement park that had go-cart racing, a mini train ride, and bumper cars. All of which you could see from my porch.

Saturday mornings, my father would make his way outside so fast you would have thought the President of the United States was coming to meet him. He would sit in his chair so that he could see the eye-catching women that jogged or walked around the track. In his flip-flops, blue-jean shorts and white T-shirt, he sipped on lemonade and spit out sunflower seeds.

The week prior, he was on the phone with his friend Ron, and I remember him saying, "You need to get over here man. I see one with a nice ass. She puts my old lady to shame." I could only shake my head, frown and walk away.

As I sat in my father's chair on this night, however, I thought back to the party when a fellow classmate, Steve Wilson, uttered the unthinkable. He wanted to go out with me. Edified that he really wanted to, made me feel temporarily as worthless as crack-head Kim. I looked down at my dusty black pumps and then to my watch. It was now 11:00 p.m. I decided to call it a night.

After going inside, taking a shower and brushing my teeth, I hopped into bed. I was tossing and turning all night. Boy was I having an arduous time falling asleep. Steve Wilson? I contemplated. I don't think so. Where did he come up with the notion that I was remotely intrigued with his ugly ass? He was not only ugly as hell; he had a repulsive potbelly and bad breath. His breath smelled like doggy-do and his pores reeked with musty body odor. When I met him, I thought that he was the most detestable looking boy at school. And from the looks of those teeth of his, his religion must have denounced dental floss. He had that foul green and yellow shit in between his teeth. It looked like dried squash and collard greens. My grandma used to say, "If you don't floss everyday, you'll have a boo-boo mouth." She explained that food in between your teeth attracts bacteria, so if you don't floss daily, you will have bad breath. I hate it when people don't use dental floss, and for some unexplainable reason, Steve made it a point to smile nonetheless and speak to me at close range. Boy did that turn my stomach. Steve and every boy that I have met since, if they don't floss I nickname them boo-boo mouth. I know that sounds cruel, but hell, I had to let them know.

Talking negatively about people was not my cup-of-tea, but as I said earlier, Steve Wilson was a fucked-up looking dude. His Afro looked as though it hadn't been picked in months. It was matted down in spots and stood straight up in others. His clothes were always dingy and wrinkled. I wondered if he had parents because he was always begging for money. I couldn't fathom giving him money, let alone sleeping with him.

I really grappled with the idea that he seriously believed that he possessed characteristics that merited my affection. Am I ugly? I heeded. I know damn well that I can do better than his pitiful ass. Can't I? Eventually, I feel asleep.

CHAPTER 2

Just a month ago, I was at the pinnacle of my short-lived existence. I had recently started my senior year, accepted to Clark-Atlanta University with a scholarship in math, and dating the most incredible young man I had ever laid eyes on. I've seen a lot of young men in my time, and Steven, my boyfriend of the last two and a half years, is one of the most attractive. It didn't hurt that he was the quarterback of our championship football team. He has a beautiful mocha complexion, light brown eyes, and the most incredible skin. And he smells so good.

On my 17th birthday, Steven was taking me out to celebrate. Unfortunately, my celebration turned into a catastrophe. That no-good-son-of-a-bitch dumped me! How could he? I'm the irresistible Charlene Bedford! I was the queen of the prom, head cheerleader, and the person named who's who among students. He dumped me for some airhead that wants to dress manikins for a living.

Anyway, not even a week following my mishap with him I was now upstairs in my bedroom with someone else. Now don't get me wrong, I wanted to work things out with Steven, but that jackass wanted nothing to do with me. What was I supposed to do? Wait to see if he would come around? Was I doing this to get back at him? Or was I doing this because I really wanted to? "Hell, I wanted to!"

I lay across my bed. As my white ceiling fan turned ever so slowly, the most erotic breeze filled my room. As I looked around at the off-white walls, my poster of Prince on his motorcycle, and then my burgundy bed spread, the sounds of Janet Jackson's *VELVET ROPE* CD filled my head.

With every breath, the scent of jasmine candles filled my lungs. All I could think was, *is this is really happening?* I couldn't believe that I was letting someone else go where only Steven had gone before. I closed my eyes and let the soothing touch caress and take over my entire body. All I could think was *God this is pure ecstasy.*

As our lips and then our tongues united, passion coupled with adrenaline took over. "Don't stop" is all that could escape my lips. I inhaled the aroma of our bodies with the mixture of the scented candles, and got turned on even more. I didn't know my body could feel this way. It was all about me, satisfying me, pleasing me, catering to me. With Steven it was "come on girl," and it was over before I knew it.

Never knew love could be like this- Oooo! I enjoyed strong, yet firm hands, caressing my perfectly round breast and moving slowly down my lean body, exploring other areas. The long, hot, sensual kisses on my full voluptuous lips, continued to send chills throughout my body. It was electrifying! Soft, yet strong hands gripped my waist, while my erect nipples were being stroked, pinched, pulled and licked with the most sensual overtone. I gripped the sheets and lightly bit my lower lip from the pleasure.

Slowly kissing down to my stomach, my firm thighs opened like a rose blooming and ready for the plucking. "Pluck me," I said under my breath. While my eyes were still closed, I felt fingertips softly tracing my precious flower and then one entered me slowly, in and out, over and over again. As the soft, moist tongue eventually became lost between my legs, abruptly, the hand that gave me life opened the door to my room.

"Baby girl I'm home," Dad said as he pushed the door to my room completely open. "What the fuck is going on in here!" Dad said as he caught me naked engaged in my first lesbian experience. "Get your head from between my daughter's legs!" Dad said fiercely. "You are not going to earn your lick-her license here!" Dad shouted. "Charlene, you and your carpet munching slut need to get out of my house right now!" Dad demanded as he waited at the door for Stacy and me to get dressed and leave. My face turned white with wrath.

"I'm sorry daddy. Please don't kick me I out," I said weakly.

"Get out now!" he declared.

That wasn't the hoped-for answer. I was hurt, embarrassed, and ashamed. But damn, the loving was good! I had no idea that my father was in the house nor did I think that he would become so hostile. The old morals that he grew up with, didn't lend any sympathy to my desire to be happy or in love. Heck, I'm not sure whether he would have responded much differently if he had caught me in bed with a boy.

After dad barged in on me, so many things were running through my head, suicidal thoughts among others. My mother unfortunately passed away while giving birth to me. Dad was all I had. I loved my dad dearly, but on that day, he vowed to never speak to me again...

CHAPTER 3

My mother named me William after my paternal grandfather, William J. Cole Jr. The only similarity between my grandfather and I was our name. He was very religious and I was far from it. I was a heathen in every sense of the word.

One day while sitting on my bed, I was reading a Morehouse College brochure. I was daydreaming of the fun ahead of me, when I heard my mother's voice.

"William, telephone," she yelled. "It's Robert, and dinners almost ready. Don't be long."

"Okay!" I yelled downstairs to her.

"Yo, man what's up?" I asked after picking up the receiver and noticing that my ringer was off.

"Man did you get your package from Morehouse today?

"Yup," I replied.

We're going to be college men in a month can you believe it?" Robert asked.

"Not really. I'm just glad that we're going to be roommates," I said.

"William, dinners ready," Mom yelled again from the bottom of the stairs.

"Man I got to go. Moms got dinner ready and you know how she is about the family thing."

"Yeah, hit me back later," Robert said hanging up.

I grabbed my navy blue NIKE T-shirt from the foot of my bed, and threw it on my 6'1" frame. I stopped at the mirror and thought *damn I look good!* When I reached the dining room my mother and eight-year-old sister, Monique were already seated at the table. My mother Gwen, a beautiful 5'5" petite coca brown complexioned woman, smiled when she saw me enter the room.

"Where's pops?" I asked sitting down next to my sister and leaning over to mess up her hair. Monique just pushed me back and smiled. I looked over at my mother and noticed the smile and the gleam in her eyes disappears.

"He's working late," my mother said looking down placing a piece of fried chicken on her plate. I reached over and touched my mother's hand, which was still on the platter of chicken. My mother looked into my eyes and laboriously smiled. She hoped it would ease my mind, but it didn't.

Monique was not paying my mother or me any attention she was too busy piling green beans, macaroni and cheese and corn muffins on her plate. She had to hit me in the arm twice to get my attention to pass the chicken.

"For the last time, could you please pass the chicken? I think you have gotten acquainted with it long enough," Monique said with her hand extended for the platter. I was so deep in thought about my father missing yet another family dinner that it was like coming out of a trance when I finally acknowledged that Monique was talking to me.

"About time, a girl could starve to death waiting on you," she said after I placed the platter in her hands.

I fixed my plate and ate quietly. My mother was trying to make light conversation, but I didn't feel like conversing and all Monique could say was; will you pass this or will you pass that. I looked at my sister and thought *for someone to be so small she sure could put away a lot of food.* We ate and ate some more.

Some six hours following dinner, pops was still not home. My mother and sister had been asleep for hours, but I waited.

When my dad did eventually come home, I heard the front door open and the sound of his briefcase hit the floor. I cleared my throat to let him know that he was not alone. My father, Joseph, walked into the living room and saw that I was still awake.

"What's the matter son? Why aren't you in bed? And why are you sitting in the dark?"

"Where were you?" I asked. "I heard you tell mom this morning that you would be home for dinner."

"What's your problem?" my father stated angrily.

"Look pops, you are barely in our lives as it is. Surely you could at least make it for Mom's Thursday night family dinner."

"What do you mean I'm barely in your lives?" Dad stated now raising his voice. "I see you everyday boy!"

"That's not the point, dad. You don't spend quality time at home. It's as if you are seeing another woman or something. You are never here."

"I would never cheat on your mother, son, and I ought to whip your ass for saying something like that to me. I'm working hard to keep my business going, so your mother can continue to stay at home and keep you and your sister grounded. My plan was to someday leave this business for you and your sister to take over. Monique has made it clear that she wants no part of the business, so I was leaving it to you."

"If the business is going to keep me from being in my family's life, you can keep it," I stated staring at my father.

"Watch your tone with me son," Dad stated. "I've been there for all of you."

"Financially, yes, physically and emotionally, no," I stated not moving my eyes from my father's face.

"I have done the best I can to be a good father to you and Monique."

"What about a good husband to mom?" I asked. "You should have seen how beautiful she was tonight. All made up for you, and you couldn't take one lousy hour out of your day to spend with your family? If I'm not mistaken you don't have to punch a clock or have to ask someone for time off."

"I don't appreciate what you're insinuating son," Dad said. "If you can't respect me, you will have to leave my house."

My Mom heard all the commotion and came downstairs. She walked into the living room and saw Dad and me frowning at each other.

"Joseph, what's going on?"

"Your son has lost his mind, questioning my whereabouts, that's what. I've told him that if he can't respect me then he has to leave my house."

"Look, we just need to sit down and talk this out," Mom suggested grabbing dad's hand and reaching for mine.

"There's nothing to talk about. Your son feels that I'm not here for the family and I do nothing but break my back for this family," Dad said snatching his hand from Mom's grip.

"Joseph, please, can we sit down and work this out?" Mom pleaded.

"No, Mom, there is nothing to work out," I stated. "I feel that pops is wrong for not being there for us in the past and for not being here now," I said walking up the steps leading to my room.

"William, please, he is your father," Mom said now crying.

"Let him go. He wants to say man things, let him try living in a real man's world," Dad said as he made it to his room and slammed the door.

"Joseph, I can't believe that you are putting our son on the streets," Mom said after opening my parent's bedroom door and closing it behind her.

Monique was standing at the top of the stairs listening and crying. "William you can't leave me, who's going to watch over me now?" Monique asked grabbing me around my waist and burying her wet face into the lower part of my chest.

"You will always be my little Mo-Mo and I will always be there for you." I told her.

I went to my room and pulled out the new luggage my mother purchased for me as part of my graduation gift. I began pulling my clothes out of the closet and throwing them on the bed.

"Mama you've got to do something. Will is packing his clothes," Monique said running to my mother's side.

"Calm down baby and let me talk to your brother for a minute," my mother said as she came into my room.

"Look son, it's late. Both you and your father said things that you didn't mean. Let's try to get some sleep and talk about this calmly in the morning," mom stated as she hugged me.

"Mom, I meant everything I said," I stated as I broke from my mother's hug so I could see her face. "You have been the one raising Mo-Mo, going to my baseball games, and throwing the football with me. You got Mo-Mo involved in ballet, doing bake sales, and car-pooling. You were on the PTA at my school and Mo-Mo's, and you were the best neighborhood mom ever. Every kid felt at home when they came over here."

"Son, I was able to do all of those things because of your father's hard work. That is how I could be there for you and your sister," Mom stated as she gently touched my face.

"Maybe pops working hard did allow you to be there for us, but that's no excuse for him not ever being there. Easter, Thanksgiving and Christmas were the only times we knew for sure that he would be home. That's the sad truth, three days out of 365. Mom that's just not right."

"Son, please don't go, we will get through this. You only have a month left before you leave for school and I don't want you to leave this way," Mom pleaded.

Without saying a word I began packing my bags. I knew that only an apology, that I was not going to give, could fix what had occurred. Monique stood in the doorway of my room and cried while my mother leaned against the dresser and released an uncontrollable cry. I packed enough clothes for three weeks.

"Mom, I'll be back to pack up the rest of my things before leaving for school," I said as I picked up the over stuffed bag. I hugged and kissed my mother on the cheek, walked over to my sister and did the same.

"Will, please don't go," Monique pleaded as tears streamed down her brown sugar complexioned skin, her light brown eyes red from crying.

Without saying a word, I headed downstairs. My mother and Monique followed close behind. During all the commotion, they hadn't noticed that my Dad had come back downstairs. He wanted to see with his own eyes if I would really leave.

In unison, both Gwen and Monique pleaded with Dad to stop me from leaving. Dad was sitting in the dark living room with his back to the door facing the window that looked out on to the driveway.

"Let him go!" Dad yelled.

I put on my jacket, grabbed the keys to my red 1996 Honda Civic, off the table, picked up my bag and headed out the door. Mom and Monique left Dad downstairs, alone. Dad sat in the dark and wept.

I drove around trying to figure out where to go and what to do. I slept a while, drove a while. After driving around aimlessly, I found myself in front of my best friend Robert's house. I looked at the time on the dashboard and noticed it was 8:30 in the morning. Unlike my parents, both of Robert's parents worked. Robert was home alone.

Robert was an only child and it's amazing to me that I would see his father at all due to the fact that he drove an eighteen-wheeler from state to state. His father was always in attendance at Robert's sporting events and anything at the school that needed a parent's involvement. I was definitely envious of that. My dad was right here in the city and had an excuse for everything.

Robert's father threw the football with him every chance he got. That's why he's going to Morehouse on a football scholarship.

My father just didn't understand. Yes, I gained financially, but lost out on what could have been a special father/ son relationship.

I must have sat in the car for what seemed to be an eternity, reminiscing about my father. I don't even remember getting out of the car, but there I was banging on Robert's door like there was no tomorrow. I heard Robert yelling from the other side.

"Stop ya banging, I'm coming!"

Robert snatched the door open and yelled, "What!" before he saw that it was me.

"Man, I'm sorry if I woke you," I stated.

"Naw man it's ok. But had it been anybody else, they would have gotten their ass whipped," Robert replied opening the door wider so I could enter.

I forced Robert a smile and walked in.

"Man you look like hell, what happened to you?" Robert asked with a concerned look.

"Pops and I got into it last night and he kicked me out," I stated.

"You have got to be kidding!" Robert exclaimed. "Come on in the den, so we can talk."

I followed Robert into the den. I sat in the plush blue recliner and let out the footrest like I had done so many times before. Robert lay on the blue leather sofa and pulled a small gray blanket on top of him.

"Now tell me, what happened between you and your dad?" Robert asked.

"To make a long story short, pops missed another family dinner and I confronted him about it. His whole non-relationship with me and the rest of the family," I stated as I closed my eyes trying not to cry.

"Man, I'm sorry to hear about what happened. I'll talk to my parents about you staying here until it's time for us to leave for school," Robert added.

CHAPTER 4

I awakened to a scorching 92 degrees. The glare from the sun hit my eyelids like a flashlight in the middle of the night. Within seconds, my eyes were squinting trying to achieve clarity. The heat from the sun suggested that I either lay in anguish, or get out of bed. I chose the latter. Decked-out in my long white T-shirt and no panties, I crawled out of bed. I can still recall my Grandma saying, "Sleep without panties Tanya, unless it's that time of the month. A lady has got to let her body breathe."

I pushed my rainbow colored covers down around my feet, mistakenly pushing my baby lion stuffed animal to the floor. I stretched my arms above my head, yawned, and shifted my feet to the teal green carpet. I tasted the sourness in my mouth and felt the fluid in my bladder. I slipped on my pink bedroom shoes and moseyed along to the bathroom.

My bathroom was directly across from the foot of my bed and ornamented with my favorite colors, lavender and gray. My towels and shower curtain were lavender and the rug on the vinyl flooring was a beautiful charcoal. After relieving my bladder, I reached over into the tub and turned on the shower.

After bathing, flossing, and brushing my teeth, I arched my eyebrows. I then, hot curled my hair and put on a dab of make-up. After getting all-cute, I put on my skintight Jordache jeans. I couldn't wait to start my day!

I was to meet Donna, at 19 Old Fulton Street in Brooklyn, the home of Grimaldi's Pizzeria. Our parents were going to transport us over the beautiful Brooklyn Bridge and drop us off at the restaurant at noon. Donna told me that adorable boys from other schools started hanging out there on Saturdays. I hadn't been in a while so I was really looking forward to it. I was hoping that the ugly curse would rid itself from around my neck so that I could be united, at last, with my prince charming.

Grimaldi's was my favorite place to eat. When you walk in, you are always greeted and seated promptly. It was a nice, yet cozy restaurant that had red and white checkerboard-print tablecloths, pictures of Pavarotti, Sinatra and Brando covering the walls, and nine times out of ten it's either the voice of Old Blue Eyes or the Italian tenor that emanates the jukebox. Although I'm not Italian, I feel like I am among family.

The pizza is scrumptious. The crust is thin and crisp, thick redolent fresh sausage along with strips of roasted red peppers are the main ingredients; and the homemade mozzarella, which is dropped in small gobs on the sauce, is the perfect final touch. Pizza has simply never tasted so good!

Now that I had exited the shower and gotten dressed, I made my way to the kitchen to make me something to eat. I opened the refrigerator, took out some eggs, cheese, grits, and bacon. I opened the loaf of bread that was on top of the microwave and put a couple of slices in the toaster. After eating cereal all week, I wanted to have a real breakfast for a change. I decided to cook for my parents as well. I scrambled some eggs and tossed them in the frying pan. I adding cheese and sprinkled a little salt and pepper. I turned on a supplementary burner and put on the bacon. I put on a pot of coffee and boiled hot water for the instant grits. Within a minute-or-so, the toaster sprang up two lightly browned pieces of toast.

"Good morning, Honey," mom said as she came into the kitchen.

"Oh, hey mom, I didn't hear you come in," I said with laughter in my voice. "Did you sleep well?"

"I slept alright. What about you dear?"

"It was a little rough falling asleep at first, but eventually I fell asleep. Slept like a baby."

"Good dear. I'm glad you slept well."

"Where's dad?"

"He said he was going to jump in the shower and be right down."

"Well, as you can see, I have already started breakfast for you guys."

"Well, that was awful thoughtful of you."

"You know I'll do just about anything for my folks," I said. "We should be eating in a few minutes."

Just as I heard the water shut off in the shower, I yelled to my father, "Come and eat daddy!"

"I'll be down in a second," he shouted back.

I went to my room, slipped on my red bedroom shoes, and went outside to get the newspaper. Just as I came back inside, my dad graced us with his presence. I handed my mom the paper and began setting the table.

"Good morning, daddy."

"Good morning, pickle head. What do you have planned for today?"

"Mom's going to take me to Grimaldi's later."

"Well, have a good day today sweetheart."

"I will, dad."

During breakfast, it was so quiet that you could hear the clock ticking on the wall. Mom was reading the paper while sipping on coffee. Dad was never a man of many words, and this morning was no exception.

After breakfast, I turned on the television. To my dismay, there was a news flash informing the community that a storm was en route. When I went outside earlier to get the paper, I didn't pay much attention to the dark clouds that hovered above. I assumed that it was merely the transition from night to day.

Unhesitatingly, I decided to go outside and see if I could determine where the storm was coming from or more consequentially, where it was headed. I was hoping that it would pass over us. I opened my front door and from my porch, I could see caliginous clouds moving toward me. The gloomy overcast put me in an impetuous state of depression. I was really looking forward to going to the restaurant. I noticed that the windows were down on my father's car, which was parked in the gravel driveway on the side of our house. I ran back to my room, slipped on my white Reebok tennis shoes, and hurried out to the car. Once back inside, I kicked off my shoes, made my way over to the sofa, and called Donna.

"Hey girl, have you seen the news?" I said as a gnat flew in my eye.

"No. What's wrong?" Donna asked.

"It looks like a storm is on its way. It appears that it's going to rain most of the day so we are going to have to cancel our plans," I said reluctantly as I wiped my eye with my index finger.

"That's okay. You sound like someone died or something," Donna said with a bit of sarcasm.

"I know, girl. I was really looking forward to Grimaldi's, you know, seeing all the fine boys and all. I also wanted to talk to you about something or should I say someone at school."

"What happened at school? Is everything all right?"

"Well it didn't really happen during school hours, it happened at the party last night. Steve Wilson told me that he had the hots for me."

"Yuck. Did you vomit, when he said it?" Donna asked.

"I barely slept a wink last night."

"I'm not sure that I understand. Do you like him or something?"

"Very funny! Hell no! I'm just wondering why the cute boys don't think that I'm attractive?" I said.

"I'm sure they do. It's just that their ego won't let them approach you," Donna said.

"What does their ego have to do with it?"

"Let me ask you this. Do you smile or wink at the boys you like?" Donna asked.

"No," I replied.

"That's the problem."

"How so?" I inquired.

"Boys want you. Trust me. They need to know that you like them before many of them will ever approach you," Donna added.

"When did you become the expert on how to attract boys?"

"I'm no expert. A while back, I overheard my brother talking to some of his friends. And you know they consider themselves to be "all that," right?"

"Yeah, and?"

"That's what I heard them say."

"So let me get this straight. Men approach women, but girls have to approach boys?"

"When I asked my mother, Ms. Sociology professor, about that a week or so ago, she said that men are pretty much the same way."

"Wow. That's not what I'm used to seeing," I said.

"Well, I didn't think so either. Mom broke it down like this: Most men approach women that they feel will be an easy score. You know, the ones that they think come a dime a dozen."

"Average looking girls?" I asked.

"You got it. That way if the lady doesn't want them, it won't be a major blow to their ego. You know that males have huge ego's right?"

"Yeah," I said with agreement in my voice.

"Mom says it's like buying a car."

"Buying a car?" I asked confused by the comparison.

"Yeah, let me explain. She used this example: You know that you want that red convertible Mercedes, but you feel that you don't have what it takes to get it. Therefore, you settle for something that is easy to get. Yes, it meets your transportation needs, but it's really not what you want and it didn't take much to get it."

"You know, I never looked at it like that. Your mom appears to have it all figured out."

"Oh, she does girl. She also believes that marriages fail for that same reason," Donna stated.

"How so?" I solicited.

"She said that most men settle for consistent sex, not love. That is why married men cheat on their wives."

"Why don't married men stay at home and have sex with their wives all the time?" I asked.

"Girl, you're asking me all of the same questions I asked mom. She said that since the man has never been crazy about his wife in the first place, he treats her like shit. Invariably, the wife is rarely in the mood for sex because of the way he treats her. Invariably, you like that word huh? Mom taught me that one."

"Girl, you're a trip," I said.

"I know. So anyway, the woman a man is cheating with doesn't have to be attractive or anything like that, her only qualification is that she is willing to do it."

"Wow! My mom and I don't talk about stuff like that."

"My mom and I didn't either until I brought it up," Donna added.

"Hey we need to talk more about this, but for right now I need to get off this phone. I want to continue watching the news to see when this storm is going to let up. I'll call you back."

"All right girl. Call me later. Bye."

Just as I sat down on the couch and continued watching television, a bolt of lightening came blazing through my living room window. With a loud BANG! My family's eleven-year-old television was annihilated.

"Daddy!" I screamed, as I watched the smoke from the television rise to the ceiling.

"What in the hell is going on?" Dad asked as he and mom entered the room. I began explaining what had happened as we searched for the fire extinguisher, while putting out the fire.

The winds began to pick up even more. The winds were so strong that it sounded like dogs howling. I became startled when the branches of a sleeping willow tree started banging up against the side of the house. Faintly, I could hear trees cracking. I looked out my living room window and witnessed a horrendous downpour of rain and leaves being hurled in the air. Screen doors from my neighbors' houses were slamming open and the electrical power was slowly fading. I was completely bewitched by the exceptionally fast paced destruction this storm was inflicting. It looked as though this storm was never going to let up.

My mom, dad, and I worked as hard as we could to keep the rain from coming in but to no avail. The rain became too much for the city's sewage system and began flooding our home. My house was loosing power and we now had more than three inches of water. As the water was filling our basement, my parents and I took buckets full of water and poured them down the sink. We did our best to keep the water from rising any higher.

It rained for three days and flooded the town like never before. Luckily, the water only flooded the basement of our home, and not the kitchen or bedrooms. Water in some places reached heights of four feet. Twenty-six people died in this travesty while hundreds lost nonreplicable memorabilia.

My next-door neighbor, Mr. Simmons, was so sick that he was coughing up blood. Doctor's offices were swamped with patients complaining of chest pains and diarrhea. My father appeared to have none of these ill-starred symptoms, but mom and I were two of the seventeen mirthless patients. The doctors wrote prescriptions for antibiotics to treat the flu, but for many of us, the drugs didn't work. Mom and I were sick for two weeks. At one time, I had chills and a fever of 104. I was taking Tylenol to combat my fever and finally after two weeks, my fever broke.

It wasn't whimsical then, mucus constantly dripped from our noses and our eyes looked like Mike Tyson had gotten a hold of us. Mom and I later joked about how wretched we appeared during our illness, saying that we resembled two junkies looking for a fix. We considered moving after that unfortunate storm, but after repairing a few things, we decided to stay.

***

We lived in a part of town that my father was all too familiar with. My father, Richard Brown, was born about twenty minutes from where we lived. Like his father, he grew up uneducated, an alcoholic, and a womanizer. Not even a full year after marrying my mom, I am told, he spent practically every weekend in speakeasies.

One night last year, I decided that I wanted to see where my old man was spending his time. I watched as he entered the speakeasy. I was able to sneak in through the back and find a dark corner to hide in. Many of the dancers spoke to me like I was one of them. "Girl, we got a packed house tonight, we are going to make some good money," one of the dancers said excitingly.

As I gazed out into the crowd, I located my dad. He was sitting right in front of the stage, dressed in a pair of black pants and a ski blue collarless shirt. As the strippers undressed, he was shelling out dollars. He was throwing money like the Cash Money Millionaires do in their videos. He was grinning ear-to-ear as the dancers paraded themselves in front of him. My dad was now in his thirties but he acted like he was still a teenager. I hung around a while just to see how much money he was actually going to give away.

After about an hour, I saw him hand a stripper a twenty dollar bill. As she got completely naked and stated gyrating on him, I closed my eyes. I was so ashamed, I ran out of the club with tears flowing generously from my eyes, and never looked back. *But who was I to talk? I wasn't much better, I reasoned.* I have had a hard time trying to keep my dress down and my legs closed. I was just a kid, was my excuse. Dad couldn't use that one.

I found out that night though, that dad had some serious issues when it came to women. Daddy loved all women, that's what shocked me. No matter the size or color. Fat, skinny, black, white, it didn't matter. Strippers, sex, whatever, whenever was the name of the game for my old man. And although I knew of dad's sexual escapades, like many kids, you love dad just because he's dad regardless of his worldly flaws.

My dad was not very cuddly with me nor did he believe in idle chitchat or father daughter conversations. He felt that my being a girl was essentially mom's burden to teach me what it meant to be a woman. Sometimes I felt that if conceivably I were a boy, he would have been more involved in my life.

He would always come home from the speakeasy, hung-over. Moreover, when he did, you had better watch out! For a man who would slap my mother if she solicited his whereabouts, I knew not to go there. My dad was a clone of Billy D. Williams, minus brains and charm.

My mother, the former Cathy Davis, was a small television station reporter, and damn good at what she did. She was sending resumes everywhere in hopes of signing a major deal with a larger network. At the time, she wasn't having much luck. She stood 5'6" and weighed about 125 pounds. She was very petite as you can tell. She was often compared to Diane Carroll, but of course, I thought my mom was prettier.

With my father always out on the prowl and my mother unceasingly trying to chase down her next story, I spent a lot of time at home alone. I guess mom made a little money, but because of my father blowing all of his, mom had to pay for everything.

I had plenty of time, being alone that is, to tap into my artistic side. When I turned twelve, I realized that I wanted to open my own business. I knew that I wanted to speak to people but I was unsure of what I wanted to speak about. I thought about politics and considered the ministry. However, those forums weren't necessarily what I wanted. I knew what, when, and how to say something to brighten someone's day. I needed a platform that was more conducive to that type of career. If there were a way to converse from a motivational platform, that would be the platform for me.

Over a period of four years, I compiled over one hundred motivational speeches in my journal. I would spend several nights and weekends finding quotes and inspirational messages that I thought would show regard for my work.

My speeches would have gained reverence around the world then, according to mom, but I didn't know how to go about getting my work in the hands of those that could help me.

By the time I was seventeen, I had five different notebooks filled with speeches. My mother often complimented me on my efforts, when I read them aloud, and reassured me that someday, if I stuck with it, my speeches would be heard around the world.

CHAPTER 5

One day, after polishing a few of my speeches, my mother asked if I wanted to spend the rest of the day with her. I expressed my acceptance, and off we went. That momentous night is still ingrained in my mind.

We arrived downtown a little after 10:00 p.m. Mom and I stood outside of a nightclub on another hot New York City night. It was very humid and we were sweating almost profusely in the blistering summer heat. We were both wearing short sleeve white oxfords and beige khaki shorts. The standard uniform for mom and her crew. I could feel the sweat running down my back and could taste the salt on my lips. With her microphone and three personnel camera crew waiting, she was hoping to catch a glimpse of a high profile celebrity that wanted to discuss what was going on inside the nightclub. It was getting late, and we had been waiting for over an hour and a half. "I'll wait another twenty minutes, and then we're out of here," she said to her crew.

"Do you think one of them will ever come out?" one of the crewmen asked.

"Hell, I sure hope so," another crewman responded. "It's hot as hell out here."

Mom was not the type that usually hung around waiting on celebrities to show their faces, but dad had spent more money this week than ever before.

She told her crew, "Hey, celebrity interviews put food on the table much faster than ordinary people ever did. Needless-to-say, more viewers tune in when celebrities appear in the news, and I make a bonus for doing a celebrity story," Mom said.

My mother was told that she needed to get an interview with the singer "Minute Man" if-at-all-possible, if she wanted to make the most of her time. She had gotten word from one of her colleagues that he might be there that night.

My mother looked up at the sky, momentarily, and noticed a full moon. *This must be my lucky night,* she thought to herself. Just as she brought her eyes down to the entranceway of the club, Minute Man appeared. He was wearing black slacks, black paten leather shoes, and a black oxford button-less collared shirt. A real Mac Daddy. His shirt was opened to reveal his hairy chest and rope style gold necklace and medallion.

"There he is," one of the cameramen, voiced.

"Hey, Minute Man, can we have a word with you sir!" another cameraman yelled.

"Sure... sure. What can I do for you kind people," Minute Man replied, as he made his way over to us.

"We were hoping that you could tell us what's going on in there?" Mom asked.

"Oh, just people dancing, singing, and having a helluva good time."

"Is there anything out of the ordinary going on in there?" one of the cameramen asked.

"Well my friend, I have seen it all before. It really depends on whether you have seen what I have seen or not."

"What is that suppose to mean?" Mom inquired.

"Well, I take it that y'all are not rich?"

"Yeah, that's true. So what?" Mom said, now getting upset.

"Well, we that are, do things a little differently than you do."

"Like what?" Mom said now frowning with one eyebrow raised.

"Well, I will tell it to you like this. I don't work for anybody and frankly I don't have to work at all. People like you want to talk to people like me so you can feed your starving families. I feel sorry for you, but hey, it's your decision to be dumb not mine."

"What in the hell does that have to do with what's going on in the club? But not that you have mentioned it, are you saying that everybody that has to work for a living is an idiot?"

"You got it. I bet you complain all the time about your job, now don't you?"

"Why are you saying this to me?" Mom said now crying.

"Well, obviously you and this ridiculous looking crew of yours were waiting on someone like me, who enjoys life, to talk to."

"Let's get out of here!" Mom yelled to all of us as we packed up and headed towards the car. When we got home, I could see that the interview had really gotten to mom. I asked if she wanted anything to drink and she shook her head in opposition, but did not say a word.

She was sitting on our old blue couch, looking down at the glass coffee table that was covered in dust. Looking at the dusty table reminded her of how her life really was. My mother and I were very devastated at what Minute Man had said to us. I was sixteen at the time so I felt as though he was not talking to me directly, because I was too young to be well-to-do. I knew that my mother had been around long enough though, that if she had made the right decisions when she was younger, she could probably be rich by now. For the rest of the night and early the next morning, my mother did not say a word. It was one thing to be bad-mouthed by my father, but it was another to be told that you were nothing by someone that she was in awe of.

"What do you think about what that jerk, Minute Man had to say?" My mother inquired later that next evening.

"Oh, I don't know mom. I feel that he is very lucky to be where he is. He was definitely wrong about saying that to us. You are not a bad person just because you have to work everyday."

"Yeah, but if I were rich, I wouldn't have to take the shit I take off of your father. Nor would I have to be subjected to interviews like that one."

"Yeah mom, but being rich doesn't mean that you are better than anyone else."

"Yeah, tell that to the rich people. The ones that get to sign autographs, wear what they want, eat what they want and date who they want. The rest of us have to settle for jackasses like your father. The only reason I'm still married to your father is to make sure that I can feed you, get you through school, and keep a roof over your head. I hate it here! Lord knows I wish I could be married to a rich man who loved and cared about me and one that would be more of a father to you."

The quiet, self-conscious mother I once knew, was no more. Mom started coming home after work, ranting and raving about my father. If looks could kill, my dad would have been a dead man. Minute Man really did a job on her. He opened her eyes to the fact that she was accepting an unfulfilled, hopeless existence. Now, almost without exception, when mom and dad made it home from work, the circus began.

"Your being a loser is affecting the entire family. You half-ass work and you constantly stay in the streets. I should have gotten rid of your sorry ass a long time ago!" Mom shouted.

"Why don't you leave then? I ain't perfect and yo ass ain't either. I have paid the bills and have put food on the table. What more do you want bitch?"

"You don't pay for a damn thing. I want and deserve a lot more. And don't call me a bitch."

"Just like a damn woman, complains about every god damn thing. Can't you be happy with what the fuck I'm already doing for you and my daughter?"

"You just don't get it, you sick son-of-a-bitch. You cheat on me motherfucker, I know you do, and you're a damn drunk! How twisted are you? Do you think I'm supposed to be happy about that shit?"

"Go to hell, bitch!"

"No, you go to hell. And when you get there, tell that no-good father of yours I said hello," Mom said frantically as she departed the room.

My mother was contemplating divorce. The strain of feeling like a failure took such a toll on my mother that she looked well beyond her forty-four years. During that time, my self-esteem was so low that my mother suggested that we all go and see a psychiatrist to deal with family as well as individual issues. My father and I agreed. We were either going to seek help, or something bad was going to happen, I anticipated.

There we were, my fathers on one end of the couch, my mother on the other and me in the middle, as usual. Dr. Branson was an elderly psychiatrist. I would say he was about seventy. His gray hair was thinning on top and he walked slouched over as though he couldn't stand up straight. He wore glasses with those thick Coca-Cola bottle lenses, and his right eye lost its muscle control and kinda did its own thing. He had beady eyes nonetheless, and heavy connecting eyebrows. A very hairy character perfectly describes Dr. Branson. I could not tell where his hairline stopped and the hair on his back began. He looked like a miniature grizzly.

On our visit, he was adorned in his long white medical jacket.

"Well, Tanya," he began, "you know that your parents have hired me to help all of you through this difficult time and your parents have made it clear to me that divorce is imminent. Divorce is never a good thing for children. Your parents want to make sure that everyone is going to be okay when this is over." He glanced over at my parents to see if they were in agreement with his opening remarks. My mother smiled and nodded her head in agreement, as did my dad. He continued, "I have a daughter named Karen. She was sixteen when her mother and I divorced. She cried for months about our breakup. Therefore, I certainly don't want you to think for a moment that I can tell you that everything is going to be all right before you know it. My daughter is still struggling with it now and she's in her thirties."

"What do you mean struggling with it?" I asked.

"Well, she still says things like, I wish you and mom would have never broken up. Especially around the holidays, it's very hard on her. I live here, but her mom lives in Texas now. So during the holidays she has to travel to both places."

"Is that her picture on your desk?" I asked.

"It sure is. She just started wearing her hair short like that. Last year she dyed it blond and wore it very curly on top, now as you can see, she wears it like G.I Jane."

"She's cute. She reminds me of Toni Braxton."

"Who?" the doctor asked.

"She's a singer."

"Oh. Okay."

"Tanya is a very strong and mature girl," my mother said in my defense as she interlaced her fingers and rested them on her stomach. "We'll make it through this with your help doctor."

"There's no doubt in my mind that all of you will be fine, but it's going to take some time. Tanya, what I want to make you aware of is that you have the right to decide which parent you want to live with. Normally the children live with the mother and the father has visitation rights. You are practically grown now, so the decision is all yours. Your parents may not like me too much for saying this, but it is your decision to let the courts know whom you prefer to live with. I'll support you no matter what that choice may be, and so will your parents." The doctor turned his head toward my parents, but this time neither one of them were smiling.

My mom was thinking *my child would live with her dad over my dead body. Her father disrespected me and he will never treat my daughter that way.* Doc quickly brought his eyes back to me. "So you do understand what I am trying to tell you?"

I understood the good doctor all right I was merely baffled out how vastly my life was changing. "Yes, I do, doctor," I responded. I thought to myself, *how in the world was I to decide which parent to live with. I loved them both so very much. Mom loved me to death, and I guess dad did too in his own way.*

"Mom, do I have to decide? Why can't you and dad stay together for at least another year?" Before my mother could say anything, my father spoke and what he was about to say was going to shock us both.

"I know that I have always been hard on you, but that was because I've seen so many girls grow up with little or no respect for themselves or anyone else for that matter. Now don't get me wrong, I'm not perfect, but I always wanted you to be the opposite of me. I chased women for years, as you and your mom know, but I never wanted you to be caught by men like me. If there is any good in me, it's you. It's over between your mother and me. It has been over for a long time. It would hurt me dearly not to see you everyday, but baby, the decision is yours," my father said.

"Oh mama," I cried. As I got up and ran out to the car. Dad and mom followed. Session over!

CHAPTER 6

Dad gave mom the Ford Escort and the house in the divorce. Mom would let me use the car whenever I wanted to see dad. Dad went out and bought a used pick-up truck.

Now that my parents were divorced, I decided that I would alternate weeks spent with them. I definitely didn't want either parent feeling as though I loved them any less. It was the summer before my senior year and I knew things were going to be much different now. Juggling school and this unfamiliar family life was going to take some getting used to.

I decided to enroll in two summer school classes to relieve some tension. I enrolled in two easy electives; tennis and weight training. I figured these classes would improve my hand and eye coordination, tone up my body, and improve my grade point average. These classes would also help me get my mind off my parent's divorce.

I began the classes and within two weeks, I was feeling much better. I wanted to build some muscle in my arms and legs and firm up my butt and breast. I had the remainder of the summer to pull myself together. I didn't know if the summer school classes would be enough to relieve my built up anxiety but I did know that Julian Whitaker, wanted to give me an option. Julian Whitaker was a handsome young boy that I was told had an interest in me. Of course, I didn't know for sure so I smiled at him one morning following weight training. After that smile, he spoke to me at least three times a day. He would make it a point to run out of his classroom when the bell rang to catch a glimpse of me as I exited one of my classes. This ritual of his continued up until the day summer school let out.

Now that summer school was over, Julian would drive his yellow Volkswagen bug to my house. He only lived two blocks from me. He would stop right at my driveway and blow the horn. He would remain in the driveway until I waved at him from the bay window. I thought to myself, *Steve Wilson, eat your heart out.*

One day while mom was out; I had just gotten out of the shower and put on my gold panties and black bra. I covered myself with my pink cotton robe and headed outside to get the mail. Julian pulled up. For some strange reason, I felt as though I really needed to talk to him. I asked if he wanted to come in. He pulled his car in the driveway, got out, slammed the door, and nearly ran me over getting to the front door. I knew he wanted me but I surely didn't expect him to be so aggressive. After we went inside, I closed the door and led him to the living room.

"Where's your mom?"

"She's working. She won't be home until later."

"That's good to know. I surely don't want your mother to kill me for being over here."

"My mom's cool. She wouldn't be bent out of shape if she were to come home right now. Do you want to listen to some music?"

"Okay."

"Let's go to my room," I said as I led him there.

As we entered my room, I continued our conversation. "Sit on the bed and make yourself comfortable. I'll just be a minute. Let me pop in this Silk CD. Would you like something to drink?" I asked as I pushed the play button on my CD player.

"Sure," he answered as the lyrics "Freak Me baby" echoed through the speakers of my stereo.

"Soda or juice?"

"Soda is fine."

"I'll be right back," I said as I went to the kitchen and poured the soda in a 12-ounce clear glass.

"So tell me Julian, what is it about me that you like so much?" I said as I entered my room and handed him a half-filled glass of Coke.

"What do you mean?"

"Do you think I'm pretty? Smart? Or just someone you want to sleep with?"

"Hopefully, I can say this in a way that you don't take offense to it. I would love to sleep with you. I would be lieing if I said I didn't. However, I think that you are one of the prettiest girls in school. I would feel good or should I say, honored, just being a friend of yours."

"You still didn't say whether you thought I was smart or not."

"Please don't take this the wrong way either, but, I have never taken a class with you so I don't know how smart you are."

"All right, you got me on that one," I said with a slight chuckle. "So you really do like me?"

"Yeah, it appears that you really have your stuff together. No one at school has ever said anything bad about you. None of the guys have said that they have been with you. None-of-that."

"Oh really," I asked wondering how those two losers I had slept with, somehow kept their mouths closed.

"Yes, really. So I'm not going to mess up your reputation or nothing. I would first like to get to know you and see what happens from there."

"Well, enough with the mushy talk. What do you want to do today?"

"Oh, I don't care. It's up to you."

"Well, I told my mom that I would pick up some bread and sandwich meat at the store so maybe we can go and do that first."

"Sounds good to me," I said.

"Excuse me for a minute while I get dressed," I said as I took my black jeans and cream rayon sleeveless top to the bathroom, and got dressed. When I returned, I gathered my purse, slipped on my sneakers, and we headed to the store. On our walk there, I got to know him a lot better.

"So, what do you do in your spare time?" I asked.

"I'm very active in my church. I teach bible study on Sunday and I sing in the choir. During the week, I'm a member of the big brothers program, where I tutor young students in math and English."

"Wow. Sounds like you're pretty busy."

"I am."

"I would love to hear you sing someday."

"Would you like to go to church with me on Sunday?"

"Sure. I'll go."

***

On Sunday, I was blown away at how well Julian could sing. He was hitting notes like a true professional. He sounded like Brian McKnight. The boy could sing. After church, I met Julian's mother. She had been a schoolteacher for the past twenty-five years. I also met his father. He was a principal at one of the high schools in town. Intellectually, I thought that Julian and I complimented each other very well, but his singing ability was far superior to anything I could do.

***

When school started, I decided to keep myself busy. Although Julian and I were attracted to each other, we decided that our friendship was too precious to destroy by becoming more than friends. I told Julian of my plans to become rich and he told me that he would do whatever he could to help. Julian was an outstanding student. He and I agreed that we could help each other by proofreading each other's papers before we submitted them.

I made an appointment with one of the school counselors, to see what I needed to do to get into a good college. My counselor advised me that my 3.3 GPA was fine, but that I needed to join an academic club or get involved in extra-curricula activities. She made it clear that being a well-rounded student would increase my chances of being accepted. I always said that I would never join any of those academic clubs, but now I saw things totally different. I was now on a crash course for success. I did not want to be down on myself, like my mother and certainly didn't want to regret everything I've done, like my father. I wanted to make the world my oyster.

Destined to be somebody, I decided to work harder than ever. *My mother was going to be rich even if I had to give her the money*, I conceptualized.

CHAPTER 7

In the fall, I joined the Beta Club. This club was unique in that it was filled with eggheads that I thought were destined to attend Ivy League schools. We often debated on topics such as welfare reform, technology, presidential agendas, as well as other worldly matters. I felt somewhat strange in this atmosphere, but I knew it was what colleges preferred. I don't know, I guess I was chasing an unrealistic dream. Maybe not. I had no clue of how I was going to make all of this money but I figured if I hung out with enough smart kids, I would uncover the secret. I enrolled in economics, business statistics, and a business management course, along with two electives. I wanted to see if, just maybe, these classes had the answer I was looking for. I found myself more involved in the Beta Club then I ever imagined, and studying became a difficult yet rewarding experience. Julian was a tremendous asset. Whatever I overlooked in my papers, he was able to catch and make the right suggestions. I had made an "A" on every paper so far.

I dabbled with the idea of opening my own business after high school instead of going to college. I learned in my economics class that I needed quite-a-bit of my own start up capital if I want to succeed at the outset. I realized then that college was definitely in the cards for me.

Nearing the end of the first semester, I found myself working harder than a chicken in a chicken fight. I made good grades and was tired from all of the hard work. I thanked Julian immensely for all of his help. I always thought of myself as a rational individual, but never a nerd. I was into my schoolwork so much, that I could have easily been the poster child for "Nerds Anonomist."

I was able to increase my overall GPA to a 3.52 and was elected vice president of the Beta Club. I read somewhere that the average SAT score for the University of Miami was 1170 and from the looks of my pre-SAT results, I knew that I had quite-a-bit of studying to do.

Mom was slowly coming out of her trance and back to her old self. I spent as much time as I could, trying to take her mind off feeling-sorry-for-herself. While taking care of mom, I knew that I had only a few days to prepare for the SAT that was right around the corner. After completing my homework, I spent every evening going over practice exams in my SAT study guide.

***

Finally, the big day to take the SAT had arrived. It was a cold Saturday morning and mom and I jumped in the car and headed to the school. It was now January and the cold winters in New York got so cold, that I thought my bones would break if I bumped into something or someone. Nervous? Yes. Confident? No. Going to give it my best? You had better believe it!

Once I arrived at school, I found out where the test was being administered. Walking into the room where the test was being held was like walking to the gas chamber. I felt like the whole world was on my shoulders. I wasn't alone in feeling that way though many of the others there were saying good luck, as much as a newly wed couple hears, congratulations on their wedding day. My palms were very moist and butterflies hit me like an abandoned animal getting attacked in the wild. I was scared as hell, but asked GOD to get me through it. As I came out of my prayer, the test administrator asked if anyone needed to use the restroom or get a drink of water before we got started. My hand along with several others went flying in the air. She told us that we had ten minutes before she handed out the test. When I returned to my seat, I looked around the room to see if I saw a familiar face. Nope, not one.

I managed to pull myself together before the exam. I filled out all of the preliminary information: name, social, etc. After the proctor stated how much time we had for each section and not to guess because it would count against us, I took a deep breath. During the exam, I realized that it wasn't as bad as I thought it would be. Unsure of whether I did well enough to get into Miami or Rutgers didn't really matter that much. I knew that I had done my best, and didn't plan on taking the test again. When I got home later that morning, I told my mom all about it. She told me that I was a smart girl and not to worry.

***

"Julian, this is Tanya. Did I catch you at a bad time?" I asked after calling his house.

"No. How did the test go?"

"It went okay I guess."

"Don't worry, you did fine."

"I'm not going to worry. I'm just glad it's over. I just wanted to call and to thank you one more time for all of your help, regardless of how these SAT results turn out."

"Oh you're quite welcome. Hey I gotta run, moms calling."

"All right, call me later."

I thought about Donna and I'm sure she wanted to know how everything went. Donna was not very sure of what she wanted to do with her future. She wanted to stay at home with her mom for a while after graduation, and hadn't said anything since to the contrary. I wanted to celebrate all of my hard work by inviting Donna to Grimaldi's. It was now one o'clock, the ideal time to go.

After dialing Donna's house, I walked into the kitchen and made myself a bowl of fruit. I sliced some bananas, green apples, and peeled an orange.

"Donna?"

"Hey girl. What are you doing?"

"Eating a snack. Just wanted to call and ask if you wanted to go to Grimaldi's?"

"Heck yeah. I was wondering when we would get a chance to go. You being so busy and all."

"I've all ready asked my mom if I could use the car. She told me to go right ahead. So I'll be over there in a few minutes."

"I'll be ready."

When I arrived at Donna's house, she was wearing blue jean overalls with a New York Mets starter jacket. She always did like dressing like her brother. I had on my Gloria Vanderbilt jeans, brown cardigan sweater, and black leather full-length coat. As I approached Donna's house, I noticed her brother Ronnie, peaking out the window. Within seconds, there were at least two other boys standing at the window staring at me. Just as I began to reach for the doorbell, I heard Ronnie yell, "Donna! Tanya is here." I tucked my hand back in my pocket without ringing the bell.

"Hey Girl, come on in," Donna said as she opened the door and let me in. Ronnie and his two friends were standing in the foyer now, watching my every move. It felt like I was in a courtroom.

"Hi fellows," I said with a big wide grin."

"Hey Donna," one of Ronnie's friends said as Ronnie pushed him in my direction.

They laughed.

"Are you ready to go?" I asked Donna.

"Yeah," Donna said. "You boys need to run along now," Donna said as we burst into laughter while walking to the car.

On our way to Grimaldi's, I decided to stop at Walgreens to pick up a cheap camera and some film. I figured if I couldn't get a cute boy to notice me, I would always have a reminder of me noticing him. I enjoyed shopping at Walgreens because there was a handsome manager there named Mr. Bernstein. He was so nice. If I was ever short a few pennies or so, he would always say, "I got it. Don't worry about it." Walgreens has all of my hair needs on aisle one, my feminine needs on aisle two, and body lotions on aisle three. I loved that store. I knew where everything was and I knew that I would be able to see Mr. Bernstein.

As I sashayed through the store, it was like I was walking on air. The room temperature was about seventy-five degrees so I got a chance to take off my leather jacket and parade myself in front of him. Mr. Bernstein was engaged so I thought I still had time to change his mind. Not really. I knew he was too old for me. But it was an arousing thought nonetheless. He had to be at least thirty something. Anyway, I still had a good time flirting with him.

"Hey, Mr. Bernstein," I said seductively, batting my eyes like a groupie.

"Well hello, Tanya and Donna. What brings you young ladies to the store today?"

"I need a really good, but really cheap, camera. Donna just came with me to get it."

"This cannon is on sale. You can get a roll of film free if you purchase it."

"How much is it?"

"Twenty-four ninety-nine plus tax."

"Okay, I'll get it."

"Do you want indoor or outdoor film?"

"I didn't know there was a difference. But I'm definitely taking the pictures indoors."

Donna and I laughed.

After purchasing the camera and film, we waved good-bye to Mr. Bernstein, as we walked gracefully out the door, to the car, and on our way to the restaurant.

When we got to the restaurant, we had a blast! We laughed at some ugly guys, and took pictures of some very cute ones. I never did find Mr. Right though. Donna and I spent the next few weekends still looking for him as well as hanging out at her house.

***

When my test results finally came back weeks later, I scored a cool 1300. I was ecstatic. Mom treated me to the Olive Garden. I love their grilled chicken salad. Now with the SAT behind me, it was time to apply to colleges. I applied to, Miami, Florida State, and the University of Georgia. I wanted to attend a top-notch institution while having fun in the sun. Getting into one of these schools, I thought to myself, *I would unquestionably become rich*. I found it very difficult sleeping at night worrying about being accepted to one of these schools. Through this experience, I learned that patience was not one of my virtues.

***

About four months after I applied to colleges, my mother nearly broke my bedroom door down one Saturday morning bringing me letters from the different universities. She sat at the end of my bed and spread the letters out. I slowly sat up on the bed, cleaning the crust out of my eyes, and stared at the letters.

"Which are you going to open first, baby?"

"I don't know, Mom. Why don't I just open all of them. See which schools have accepted me, then make a decision."

"Sounds good baby. Here, let me help you."

I was accepted to all of the schools that I applied to. I decided that I would attend the University of Miami. My dream had finally come true. I was going to be a "Hurricane" for sure. I knew that my intellectual ability would undoubtedly be tested and making millions was only four years away.

Through my research about the various colleges, I found out that the University of Miami was among the 149 universities in the country with a fully accredited business school that was why it was my first choice. I called Donna to tell her about my decision to attend Miami.

CHAPTER 8

It was a Sunday morning in the late summer, the air not yet thick with steamy heat. I packed my car with everything I owned before traveling to Atlanta. I was exceptionally excited about going away to college, just as any other in-coming freshman would be.

When Robert and I made it to the campus, I was looking forward to being on my own and sowing my wild oats.

Spellman, Clark-Atlanta, and Morris Brown were a hop-skip-and-a-jump away. So I knew that I would have more prospective woman than I knew what to do with.

When I arrived on the historic Morehouse campus, I was proud to be a part of the legacy. When Robert asked, "William, do you want to tour the campus?" I responded excitedly, "You know I do!"

We toured the campus, reading every caption possible to learn more about the founding fathers of this fine institution.

What attracted me to Morehouse was the rich heritage of African Americans that have made an indelible mark on society. Martin Luther King Jr., being the most noteworthy, majored in Sociology.

We walked around the campus for nearly two hours before heading back to our room. And although I was ecstatic about being on campus, I was still on the outs with my father and what funds I did commandeer from my piggy bank, before leaving home, were fading faster than Al Gore's hopes of becoming president.

"William, you look like you just saw a ghost," Robert stated.

"Just trying to figure out how I'm going to make it through the school year," I said after we made it back to our room.

"Well, you know I'm here for you."

"Thanks man."

I have to admit, although dad wasn't there physically, he had always been there financially. Fortunately for me, dad had already paid for my first semester so I was okay for a while.

Robert told me that he had a few personal things that he needed to finish and suggested that I go to a nightclub to unwind. I decided to do just that...

CHAPTER 9

While stepping on the Clark-Atlanta campus, I felt like a little fish in a big pond. I checked into my dorm room. I found out from my dorm mother that my roommate, due to money trouble, decided to go into the military. They hadn't found me a roommate yet, so I had the room to myself. That didn't ease my feeling of being alone one bit. I went to pick up my meal card, and headed to the cafeteria. I was starved. While sitting at the table trying to eat this mess they call a meal, I realized how much I missed my father and his cooking.

In an unexcited mood, I watched the other students get better acquainted. While nonchalantly trying to be cordial to fellow students, an older well dressed woman approached my table and sat down.

"You look like you could use some company?"

"I look that lonely, huh?"

"Freshman, I take it?"

"Yes ma'am," I responded back.

"I'm Maxine Richards, she said as she extended her hand.

"I'm Charlene Bedford, pleased to meet you," I said as my hand met hers.

"Where are you from Charlene?" she asked

"I'm a New Yorker," I said proudly.

"Well, I'm from Rhode Island," Maxine said with a big smile on her face. I gave her a puzzled look as to say, what the hell is there to smile about in Rhode Island?

As she picked up on my dumb founded facial expression, she began telling me a little bit more about her hometown.

"How long have you been here?" I asked.

"Two years," she answered.

Maxine started talking about the campus, the type of students to stay away from, and some of the better professors. I wasn't sure why she was giving me so much advice, but I was listening attentively.

"Well, it was nice talking to you," I told her. "I guess I'd better get back to my room and finish unpacking. I need to prepare for classes on Monday," I said while picking up my tray.

"Maybe I'll see you around campus," Maxine said smiling at me. Maxine watched me until I was out of sight. *That woman is incredible*, I thought to myself after being out of her view.

The weekend was quiet and uneventful for me. While many of the other students were engaged in conversation about attending social mixers and parties, I had only made plans to sulk in my room.

I missed Stacy immensely and I hadn't spoken to her since my father kicked us out. In a way, I wished that day had never happened. But then again, I can't lie to myself, I enjoyed it. I just wished my father didn't catch us.

As I sat in my room, I picked up the book entitled, "Casting the First Stone." As I began to leaf through it, I was amazed at how good this book was. I read for three hours straight until I completed it. I soon thereafter, fell asleep.

Beep! Beep! Beep! My alarm went off at 6:30a.m. Oh Lord, why did I sign up for an 8:00 a.m. class? I was still sleepy and the last thing I wanted to do was get out of bed. I reached over and turned the alarm off. I got up and did what would become my usual morning routine; made my bed, worked out, and headed to the shower. As I looked around the large bathroom that I had to share with twenty-five other girls from my floor, there were only five other girls in the bathroom. I found an empty shower and placed my shower basket on the bench and headed toward the toilet stall. *Ah relief,* I whispered to myself. After taking my shower I headed back to my room to find something to wear.

It was humid as hell in Atlanta during the fall, and I had to dress appropriately. I finally found a pair of Tommy Hilfiger blue jean shorts and a red Tommy half shirt to show off my sexy abs. I put on my white K-Swiss sneakers, combed my hair back, and put my shades on top of my head. I grabbed my backpack and headed to Biology 101.

When I got to class at 7:50 a.m., there were only nine other students present. By 8:00 though, the class was packed. While I was reaching down to get my biology book out of my book bag, I heard the door close. I looked up and saw Maxine at the head of the class. *Maxine is a professor? She didn't mention that she was a professor when we talked the other day*, I reflected.

"Good morning. To make sure that all of you are in the right class, this is Biology 101. If you are in the wrong place, please leave," Maxine said forcefully as she stood by the door.

Everyone started looking around the room. A few students gathered their belonging and headed towards the door. Maxine opened the door to accommodate them.

"My name is Professor Richards. Class begins at 8:00 a.m. and not a minute later. If you get here after 8:00 you will find the door locked. After three absences your name will be turned in to the registrar's office to be dropped from my class. Does anyone have any questions?" Not a single hand was raised. "Now that we have the particulars out of the way, let's get started. Open your text and lab books to the first chapter," Maxine stated while walking around the classroom.

After thirty-five minutes into her lecture, I looked up at the clock. *Thank God, only fifteen more minutes left. Maxine seemed so nice the other day.*

"Before you leave, everyone needs to pair off. You will need a lab partner to complete a few of the assignments that I have in store for you. Make sure it's someone you think you can get along with because you will not be allowed to change partners later," Maxine stated as she sent a form around for us to sign. Everyone started looking around trying to find someone to pair up with when this cute guy approached me and introduced himself.

"I'm Robert Jordan. Would you like to be my lab partner?"

"Sure, why not," I responded with a grin on my face.

"Maybe we can get together and study," Robert said staring into my eyes, showing me his perfectly straight white teeth.

After exchanging pertinent information, I said, "Call me and maybe we can meet at the library."

"Will do," Robert said with a half smirk on his face.

"Ms. Bedford, could I see you for a moment?" Maxine asked just as Robert and I finished our conversation. I stood next to Maxine's desk and waited for everyone else to leave the room.

"So, did you enjoy the first day of class?" Maxine asked.

"I enjoyed it Ms. Richards. It seems like its going to be a tough class though. I just hope I'm able to keep up," I stated.

"Please, this is Maxine you're talking to. If you need any additional help, let me know," Maxine stated handing me a card that had her telephone number on it.

"Thank you. Hopefully you won't get mad when I'm calling your house every other day with questions," I said laughingly.

"No, as a matter of fact I'm going to start a study group at my house. Those of you that are serious about passing my class, can come over and have all of your questions answered," Maxine said.

"Good, you can give me your address right now."

"Well, I'll see you at 8:00 a.m. on Wednesday," Maxine said after handing me a slip of paper with her address. "And by the way, you look cute today, showing off your midsection an all. Wish I could get my abs that defined."

"You look great Ms. Richards. But if it makes you feel any better, I'll make a deal with you."

"What's that?"

"Help me with biology, and I'll help you develop your abs."

Maxine paused momentarily, "It's a deal."

When I registered for classes, biology was the only class that I was worried about. Now it appeared that it was going to be a piece of cake.

***

A week later, I stood at the door of this beautiful two story house. The yard was well kept with gorgeous red, yellow, pink and white roses under the windows. I rung the doorbell and waited. I heard laughing and talking from behind the door. After a few seconds the door opened and there stood Maxine in a fitted off the shoulder apple green sun dress. She was wearing matching sandals and gold hoop earrings.

She was one beautiful woman, let me tell you. She is the epitome of grace and elegance. She is smart and sexy as hell. Traffic stopper, hip popper, that's Maxine. She favors Mariah Carey, but I feel that if I compared her to anyone, it would be Lena Horne. Like Lena, she told me she was always mistaken for a much younger woman. I can't blame those that make that mistake though. She already has the mid-section of a teenager so why did she need my help? And her booty and breast are so shapely, she could start a revolution. She had to have worked out religiously to maintain her thirty-something anatomy. And if I might say so, myself, she looked damn good.

"Hello, Charlene. I was wondering if you were going to make it."

"I wouldn't have missed it for the world," I replied.

"Well come on in. The rest of the students are in the den," Maxine said as she turned to lead me there.

Thirty of the fifty-two students in the class met at Maxine's house that night, and although I mingled with the other students, I couldn't seem to take my eyes off of Maxine. She winked at me throughout the night, and I was spellbound.

The dining room table was covered with serving dishes of food. The den was very spacious with two full size white leather sofas. The sofas were decorated with overstuffed pillows in the colors of a rainbow. The coffee table was white marble with a statue of a busty woman in the center. The fire place drew your attention too it was black trimmed in gold. The mantel was covered with pictures of smiling people, and in the center of the mantel was a beautiful stained glass rainbow colored vase filled with the roses from her garden.

"Okay, everybody help yourself to something to eat and we'll get started," Maxine said heading to the dinning room.

We ate, went over study questions, and tried to pick Maxine's brain about the type of questions that we could expect on her exams.

The group session was over before I knew it and my fellow classmates started leaving. I stayed behind and started helping Maxine clean up. As Maxine put the left over food in plastic containers I started washing the platter trays.

When Maxine brushed against me to put the remaining platter trays in the sink, it was like current was passing through us. Maxine stood behind me and whispered in my ear.

"Have you ever been with a woman before?"

After being stunned by her question, I swallowed slowly. "Once," I answered as I closed my eyes and inhaled her scent of Dream Angels, by Victoria Secret.

I turned to face Maxine and she kissed me. I don't call to mind how we got to her bedroom, but there we were on her king size canopy bed. Her room was decorated in an African safari décor.

Maxine got up and lit the candles that were on her night stand and dresser. She opened the armoire, put on a *Sade CD*, and went to open the sliding glass door that led to her balcony. The scent of vanilla and the roses from her garden filled the room.

She stood in front of the door with the shears lightly blowing behind her and removed her dress. The dress hit the floor and gathered around her feet. She swept the dress to the side with her foot. There she stood wearing merely, an apple-green thong. Only the sounds of *Sade* filled the room. I watched her through the cream colored shears that draped from her canopy bed. She was so graceful. She strolled over to the beige wing back chair that was situated in the corner of her room, and sat down.

"Charlene, come to me," Maxine said in her most lustful voice. I got up from the bed and walked over and stood in front of her. Maxine unbuttoned my khaki shorts and let them hit the floor. I was uncontrollably nervous. *Is it going to be like my last encounter? Boy I'm glad that I massingaled before I came over.* She ran her hand inside my pink panties and massaged me were I hadn't been touched in months. I had so much respect for her as a professor, but what was I to think of her now? I knew that it was wrong for a student to have a relationship with their professor, but it felt so good.

As Maxine continued, my flower began to blossom with every stroke of her hand. I spread my legs a little wider to get the full effect of her fingers working their magic. My legs began to tremble and I had to grab the top of the chair to keep my balance. Maxine stopped and asked me if I was okay and I shook my head north and south, but did not say a word. My heart started racing and I couldn't catch my breath to speak. Maxine stood up turned me to where my back was to the chair and sat me down. Maxine then placed my left leg on the left arm of the chair and my right leg on the right arm. She then got on her knees and praised me in a way that had me acting like I had the holy-ghost. Maxine used her tongue and hands like an artist sculpting a master piece. I was the clay molding to her every touch, lick, stroke, and kiss. The encounter with Maxine was incredible.

"I guess you should be getting back to your dorm room so you can prepare for class tomorrow," Maxine said as she walked over to her nightstand.

"Yeah, it is getting late," I said feeling as though I was being put out. Maxine walked up to me, as I was getting dressed, and handed me a one hundred dollar bill.

"What is this for?" I asked.

"I remember how it was being a college student."

"Yeah, I guess I could use it?"

"Then take it. I'm sure you could put it to good use. I'll see you tomorrow at school," Maxine said as she led me to the front door and kissed me before letting me out.

I couldn't stop thinking about Maxine. Over the next couple of months, I spent less time sleeping at my dorm room and more nights at Maxine's. Sleeping was the last thing on our minds though, she taught me much more about anatomy than biology. Within weeks, it was like everything I owned was now at Maxine's. I learned a lot from her, about her, and about myself.

Maxine was perfect, I would oftentimes tell myself. You won't find a spot of ash on her either, lotion was her dear friend. I learned that every morning, she ran three miles, works out with weights, and does at least one hundred sit-ups, so you can imagine her "How Stella got he groove back" physique. She took half-hour showers before she applied peach scented Bath & Body Works lotion to every inch of her perfectly sculptured body.

Although she ran everyday and worked out, her skin was as smooth as a baby's bottom. I'm still trying to figure out what's taking Oil of Olay so long. They should have knocked on her door a long time ago. Did I mention that she is fine as hell? Just checking! Anyway, she has the street savvy of Queen Latifah and the intellectual prowess of Toni Morrison. She is all that and then much, much more. At first I had a problem with Maxine always buying me things and giving me money. But as she explained, if I wanted to be her lady I had to give in to her every demand. I had to trust her or go back to living the life of the poor college girl. I would do anything that Maxine asked me to do, because she's all I had and I was not about to lose her.

***

Two months to the date of our first encounter, Maxine was in the kitchen singing while stirring a pot of her delicious Spanish chicken. The aroma met me at the door.

"Baby I'm home." I said as I placed my book bag by the door.

"I'm in the kitchen." Maxine shouted back.

I walked over to Maxine and kissed her hello. She was wearing her black wrap dress and black sandals. The only jewelry that she had on was her sterling silver earrings and the sterling silver anklet with a heart charm. I had an identical set. On our anklets, had our names and the day we met. We only wore our anklets around the house.

"You sure are making a lot of food for the two of us." I said as I looked at the large salad and strawberry dessert that sat on the counter.

"We're having guest tonight. I thought it was about time you met some of my friends," Maxine said. "Why don't you go get cleaned up? They will be here in an hour."

"What should I wear?" I asked.

"A nice summer dress would be appropriate."

As I prepared myself for dinner, I was excited that Maxine wanted me to meet her friends. Maxine taught me to I floss my teeth, jump in the shower with a mouth full of Listerine, and began bathing. After about fifteen minutes in the shower, I was to towel off, spit out the mouthwash and brush my teeth with any brand of spearmint tooth. Clean teeth and fresh breath is a must in Maxine's book. I put on my gray body-fitting dress, a pair of Maxine's silver hoop earrings, and my favorite gray sandals.

An hour later, the first guests had arrived. It was Ebone, the dance instructor and her protégé, Jasmine. Ebone appeared to be in her thirties and Jasmine looked to be my age. Just by looking at Ebone, you could tell that her name fit. Her skin was smooth and chocolate. Jasmine was a petite caramel colored beauty. As Ebone walked into the doorway she gracefully hugged Maxine as if she had not seen her in years.

"Ebone, I would like to introduce you to my favorite student, Charlene," Maxine stated.

"It is a pleasure to meet you," Ebone replied. "This is my student, Jasmine."

I could not get over the fact that Maxine introduced me as her favorite student and not her girl. What was going on here? Was she ashamed of our relationship? Is this really how she sees me?

"It is nice to meet both of you," I said.

Maxine immediately escorted Ebone and Jasmine to the den and asked them if they would like something to drink. I was still in a daze, still not believing what just happened. A few minutes later, the doorbell rung again and it was Charise and Mackenzie. Both women were beautiful and stylish. Charise is a lawyer who has made partner at her firm, and Mackenzie was her paralegal. Maxine introduced me to both ladies and all I could think about was *these ladies have a lot of class. I should have known that any friend of Maxine's would be classy.*

During dinner, we sat around and talked about relationships. Ebone had come out of a bad marriage where her husband abused her. She vowed that she would never get married again. Charise was trying to convince her that that was one man and not all men were like that. Mackenzie started a conversation about men and their needs. She argued that men like women who are ladies in public but they want and need freaks in the bedroom.

"I was all that if not more," Ebone exclaimed, "that was still not enough. A person who works all day and is on the go from sunrise to sunset needs a break sometimes!"

"That's true," Mackenzie stated, "but if you don't take care of his needs, someone else will. That's why I don't want to get married. If married men are going to explore other women, then why get married? We can have fun too! Who needs to limit themselves to one person when you can try different people?"

"I know that's right," Charise said as she slaps Mackenzie a high-five.

I could not believe I was hearing all of this. I was wondering if Maxine felt this way too. Was she just using me for the moment? Or did she actually care for me and want to be with only me? They must have noticed my facial expression because Jasmine then asked me what did I think?

"Excuse me?" I asked.

"What do you think about relationships with men?"

"Well, I think that men will be men. You have good-faithful ones and then you have your dawgs. You also have another kind of lover ... a woman." I couldn't believe I was saying this to a bunch of strangers. "But I really think a relationship is what you put into it. You give nothing you get nothing."

"I disagree," Ebone proclaimed. "I gave that son-of-a-bitch all of me and that still was not enough. He wanted to control me and tell me when and where I could go. How can you respect someone that does not respect you?"

Jasmine put her hand on Ebone's trying to calm her down. "They're plenty of people, not just men, who could love you like you want to be loved or NEED to be loved," I stated as I glanced at Maxine.

"You are young and have a lot to learn about relationships," Ebone said. "But now I see why you are Maxine's new favorite student."

"We all have a lot to learn," Maxine interjected." In the meantime let's enjoy life and explore our sexualities one night at a time."

We enjoyed a delicious dinner in the dining room. Everyone was complimenting Maxine on a job well done. Maxine then said, "Charise and Ebone, lets adjourn to the den while the younger generation take care of the dishes."

As the girls are in the kitchen and the ladies make their way to the den, Charise said, "Maxine, I think Charlene is going to be down with our game."

Maxine responds, "She's not like that."

"I don't know about that, she was holding her own at dinner," Ebone interjects.

"I know my girl," Maxine said.

"I'll bet you $500.00 that she will go right along with our girls," Charise said laughingly.

"It's a bet," Maxine counters back.

"You can't tell her about the bet," Ebone instructed.

"I can do better than that. I will tell her that I want her to be a part of it and she still won't do it," Maxine replied.

"We'll see," Charise said as they crossed pinkies to seal the bet.

Later that evening, the six of us went to an upscale club, the "Velvet Room"- a known hot spot. I hadn't totally come out of the closet so the club atmosphere felt awkward. Everyone was well dressed and spending money like you wouldn't believe. "Drinks for everyone," one man yelled, while a woman, standing next to our table, offered to buy a total stranger some food. There were gay and straight men and women in the club. I had never been in such a diverse atmosphere.

As I stood beside my lady, Maxine told me that she had a surprise for me. I noticed that she was staring at a well-groomed gentleman that was standing by himself. Not only was he extremely good-looking, he was dressed in black slacks and a lime-green rayon shirt that showed off his awesome body. Maxine, along with the rest of us, started whispering to each other and pointing at the handsome man.

"Charlene, I don't think I told you, my girlfriends and I play this game with men."

"What kind of game are you talking about?"

"You'll see," Maxine countered.

Maxine got up from the table and approaches the handsome young man. "So what is your name?" Maxine asked.

"Jared," he responded.

"Jared."

"Yes," he assured her.

"My girls and I wanted to know if you would be interested in going to our place to have some fun?" Maxine asked as she pointed in our direction.

"What kinda fun? Not drugs I hope," Jared stated with a frown on his face.

"No fool, I'm talking about sex," Maxine added.

"Sex with who?" Jared asked.

"With those three younger ladies over there," Maxine said pointing in our direction again.

"What's the catch?" Jared asked

"There's no catch. They agreed that you are the best looking young man that they have seen in a long time and they all want a piece of you."

"Yeah, right. Okay, I'm ready when you are," Jared said sarcastically.

"Lets go," Maxine said as we departed the club.

Jared in his car, trailed close behind us. We were riding in Maxine's, brand new, black Lincoln Navigator when I overheard Jasmine say, "I can't wait to see this brother naked."

Once we made it inside the house, Mackenzie said, "Come with us Charlene, we have to prepare Jared."

"Prepare him for what?"

"You'll see," Jasmine stated.

I followed behind Jasmine and Mackenzie as they led Jared to one of Maxine's guest rooms. Once inside the room, Jasmine and Mackenzie began undressing Jared. Moments later, Jared stood before us in all of his glory. You could tell that he was not ashamed of his body.

"Damn you're fine." Jasmine stated as she ran her finger tips across Jared's body.

"What the hell is going on here?" I asked trying not to look at Jared, but finding my eyes drawn to his perfect body.

"We're going to have a little fun, that's all," Mackenzie stated as she pulled two red silk scarves out of the nightstand.

"What do you mean fun?"

"We're going to play a little game with Jared to see which one of us could make him cum the fastest," Mackenzie stated as she tied the silk scarves on Jared's wrist and led him to the bed.

"Girl, didn't Maxine tell you about our little game?" Jasmine asked.

"No, she didn't. And aren't the two of you involved with Charise and Ebone?" Charlene asked.

"Yes. But if you want to keep Maxine, you'd better get with the program. Just then, Maxine and the others came into the room.

Mackenzie tied Jared to the bed and blindfolded him. At first, Jared appeared to be enjoying the attention. But when Charise went over to him and whispered in his ear, "You better not cum in my bitch." He didn't appear to be too overjoyed any longer.

"I love to watch a man squirm," Maxine said.

Jared yelled, "I'm cold!"

All of them yelled back, "Shut up!" and started laughing. I looked on in amazement. I could not believe what was going on. Maxine could tell that I needed a little coaxing so she went to the kitchen and brought back shot glasses and a gallon of vodka. *I have to see if Charlene will give into the pressure, or if she's really into me, Maxine thought.*

"Here have a drink and relax. I don't want you to do anything you don't want to do," Maxine stated handing me the shot glass of Vodka.

I downed the vodka like it was water and held the glass out for another round. After about three more shots of vodka I started to unwind. I asked, "Maxine is this something you want me to do?"

"I want you to be yourself," Maxine stated staring into my eyes. *Could I really lose Maxine if I don't go through with their game like Jasmine stated?* I contemplated.

Mackenzie and Jasmine started drinking and taking their clothes off, so I took my clothes off as well. After we were all buzzing from the liquor and naked, Mackenzie said seductively, "Get the stop watch ready, I'm going first." No one said a word just shook their heads and shrug their shoulders as to say, go ahead, knock-yourself-out.

After pulling her hair back and affixing a red bow, she got on the bed with Jared and began massaging his thighs. Jared must have been an athlete because he had muscular legs and broad shoulders. As he lay there on the king size mattress that was adorned with white satin sheets, Mackenzie parted her full purple painted lips as wide as she could to take in his better than 9 inches. The man was hung like a horse, okay. I thought the girl was going to get lock-jaw. The rest of us stood around the bed holding and caressing Jared's body with big white feathers. Jared didn't know if the massaging or the blow job was turning him on the most.

Maxine had to stop her and ask, "Are you sure you're a lesbian?"

"Yes. Why?" Mackenzie asked with a shocked look on her face.

"I don't know about that girl. You look like you are enjoying that dick just a little too much my sister," she said as the rest of us started giggling. Mackenzie frowned, rolled her eyes at Maxine, got off the bed, and went and sat in the corner.

It was Jasmine's turn. Jasmine had big breast and a flat ass. You know the type. Yes, contrary to popular belief, some sister's do have flat asses. Anyway, Jasmine put a condom on Jared and got on top of him. I laughed to myself after thinking of Jared pounding her from behind. With her ass being so small, she had no cushion to absorb the pounding. He would probably rip her little ass apart, I thought, and laughed to myself again.

"Boy, you got a big dick," Jasmine said as she felt his penis going deep inside of her.

"I wish I could take this blindfold off and look at you. You are making me cum, whoever the hell you are," Jared said as he began to tremble.

"I guess that was the fastest time ever ladies," Jasmine said and started giving high five's to the rest of us.

"Well, Ms. Charlene, I think you're up next," Maxine instructed.

I was nervous as hell, but I couldn't let Maxine down. I was so happy to be accepted among her friends that I would do anything to please them. Since Jared's tool had just had a workout, I had to perform a little magic to get him ready for the next round. I untied his hands and took off his blindfold. I wanted to look into his eyes to see who I was letting into my private world. I casually walked away to down another shot of Vodka. As I approached the bed again, I began to do a sexy dance, moving my ass around and bending over so he could see my pussy. As I straddled him, I had forgotten what it was like to have a strong erect penis in my vagina. As I started to move up and down, my love tunnel began to get moist. It felt so good I had forgotten that I had an audience.

"Baby you feel as good as you look," Jared said.

"Shut up, you son-of-a-bitch and stroke my pussy like a man is suppose to!" I yelled.

Jared grabbed my breast and squeezed them so hard I got excited and started moving faster and faster as a feeling of ecstasy took over. I could not help myself as I began sucking his fingers and moaning with delight. His strokes were longer and harder then before, as if he was trying to prove something. His body felt so good I wanted more, but he lost his rhythm and I knew that I had to jump off. I did so, just in time for his love juice to squirt on my stomach.

"Bitch! You just cost me five-hundred dollars!" Maxine yelled.

"What are you talking about?" I asked dumbfound.

"I can't believe you just fucked him!" Maxine said.

"I thought that was what you wanted me to do?"

"What I want is for you to get your shit and get out of my house!" Maxine shouted and stormed out of the room.

CHAPTER 10

When I arrived at The University of Miami, I was as serious about my education as a jury convicting a rapist. I kept reminding myself, *Tanya, you have made it this far, don't blow it.*

I constantly reminded myself of that thought as I breezed through my first few years of college. I did, however, start taking a closer look at the gorgeous men on campus. My sexual hormones were in motion like Tina Turner trying to get away from Ike. I wanted to have sex and Randy Miller, a third string quarterback, was the man I wanted. He had just broken up with his airhead, over-developed, cheerleader girlfriend, Amy. He was fair game, and I was ready to play.

I knew that I was not the prettiest girl in school but far from the ugliest. I also knew that most guys would jump at the chance to sleep with me. I was still my sexy dark chocolate self. I now stood 5'6" with a very slim build. I still carried what the boys called my, "Dump truck butt."

I weighed only 135 pounds but my measurements were 36-24-40 if that gives you a better idea of how much my butt stuck out. I put a little tint in my hair to brighten it up a bit. I always wore my hair brushed straight back with my black headband. Having continued my weight training since high school, I could have easily been the president of the women's body building committee. I was smart, attractive, and had a big onion butt. "Don't hate ladies," I often found myself telling other females when their men couldn't seem to take their eyes off me. Randy, Randy, Randy, was all I fantasized about.

I had always received compliments on my eyes, so I set my sights on him. I spoke to him every chance I got, but had not yet gotten around to telling him how I really felt. Randy was a chocolate brother with beautiful brown eyes and a very muscular physique. He was tall, dark, and sexy. He was the spitting image of Michael Vick, the Atlanta Falcon's 2001 first round draft pick. There were only three months left before summer break, so I figured I had better hurry. The smile technique from the old days didn't attract Randy and the subtle hints weren't working either. I decided to be bold and just put it all on the line.

"Randy, can I talk to you for a minute?" I asked as I stood outside my dorm room.

"Sure, what's up?"

"My roommate is going out of town this weekend."

"Yeah, and?"

"I ahhhhhh, want you."

"Say what?"

"I've always been attracted to you."

"Wow! I don't know what to say."

"Well, you still haven't said you will."

"I just can't believe you asked me. Sure, when?"

"How does tomorrow sound?" I asked.

"Sounds good to me," he said.

"We'll have tomorrow and Sunday to be together, if you want to."

"Okay. What's your room number?

"I'm in room 104."

"What time?"

"Let's say tomorrow night at 8:00?"

"I'll be there."

The next morning I didn't have much money so I decided that I would go to the mall and pick up a couple of sample bottles of White Diamond. I was completely out and wanted to smell good later that evening for Randy. When I got to the mall, I ran into a fellow classmate of mine.

"Hey Leslie, what brings you out here?"

"Just came to buy a new pair of sneakers. How about you?"

"I was out of perfume."

"How did you get here?"

"I rode the bus."

"I drove. You can ride back to the campus with me if you want."

"I certainly appreciate it. I hate waiting on that slow ass bus."

"Are you finished shopping?"

"I guess so." We walked out of the mall and stepped into Leslie's black convertible mustang. She was a rich, blonde haired, blue eyed, white girl. "Would you like to get something to eat," she asked.

"I only have two dollars in my pocket, so I'll just have to wait until we get back on campus so that I can go to the cafeteria," I said.

"It'll be my treat. Now, where do you want to go?"

"Well if you're treating, McDonald's is fine."

When we returned to the campus, it was approximately two o'clock. I decided to take a nap before Randy arrived. I knew he was an athlete so I wanted to be ready for a workout. I stepped out of my clothes and into one of my long white T-shirts. I crawled into bed, set my alarm for 7:00 p.m., and fell asleep.

***

Right on schedule, my alarm clock awakened me. I got up and made my way over to my window to watch the sun set. After the sun was completely out of sight, I took off my T-shirt, slipped on my flip-flops, and threw on my blue robe. I picked up my favorite pink towel and wash cloth, a bar of Dove, dental floss, toothbrush, toothpaste, and my room key before heading to the communal shower. I walked slowly balancing all of my toiletries. When I made it to the showers I found two white girls there, brushing their teeth. I walked over to the shelves in the bathrooms and put down my pile of stuff. I grabbed my soap, washcloth and towel, and hung up my robe.

I walked to an unoccupied shower and turned on the water. After the water was desirable, I got in and pointed the showerhead directly at my chest. I lathered up my washcloth and got down to business. I washed my private parts a few more times than usual and fantasized about Randy and the ideal encounter. After finishing my shower, I flossed and brushed my teeth. I acknowledged my fellow students with merely a head nod, words unspoken.

After the oral ritual, I grabbed my pile of toiletries and I headed back to my room. When I returned, I rubbed baby oil on my body from head to toe and sprinkled baby powder on my chest. I dabbed the White Diamond perfume on my hands, before rubbing it on my neck, stomach, and inner-thighs. I slipped on my satin black bra and panties, and covered myself in my black silk robe. I decided to wear my hair down for a change. I put on a little make-up and red lipstick a couple of minutes before Randy arrived.

When he knocked on my door, anxiety took its course. I was hoping that he was not coming over to say that he had changed his mind. I know that my lure was a little overly aggressive, but what the hell; I had to have him. When I opened the door, there he was, the sexiest man I had ever had the privilege of being this close to. He was dressed in a navy blue golf shirt, faded blue jeans, and brown Timberland boots. This was definitely the total package and I was ready to unwrap him.

He had obviously gotten a hair cut earlier that day. He had one of those neatly tapered military style haircuts that complimented his face and perfectly shaped head.

"Good evening, Tanya," Randy said smiling, showing all thirty-two.

"Good evening, Randy," I replied.

"Are we still on?"

"Yes. What would make you think otherwise?" he asked.

"Nothing really, just thought I'd ask," I said as I made my way back to my bed.

"Come in. Have a seat," I instructed Randy, as I pointed to the chair by my desk.

"Damn girl, you got it going own," Randy said as he undressed me with his eyes.

"You look damn good yourself. Do you want to sit over here on the bed with me?" I said as I patted the empty space beside me.

"Sure. I don't see why not," he said as he stood up.

As Randy made his way over to me, my body moistened as he closed in. When he got to the bed I reached out for him. We hugged. He sat down.

"You smell good," Randy said.

"You smell good and you look incredible," I said sensually looking him up and down.

"Well, thank you."

I stared into his big brown eyes, feeling as though I was the luckiest girl in the world. He reached for the thin belt on my robe and I moved my hands out of his way. I stood up, lifted my robe off my shoulders, and allowed it to fall to the floor. "Wow! You are built like a brick house," he said in a low voice, like a kid opening a large present. "I knew you had a big booty, but I had no idea that you were so defined. Your body is unbelievable."

"Coming from a man as sexy as you, I flattered."

When Randy started taking off his shirt, my heart skipped a beat at the sight of his six-pack and well-developed chest. Randy stood up, took of his pants, and revealed his navy silk boxers. We gingerly approached each other and pecked on the lips. Seconds later, he gazed into my eyes, I smiled, and he kissed me again. This time, the kiss was gentle, wet, and tantalizing. As our tongues chased each other's, Randy unsnapped my bra as I began kissing him more passionately. As I took a break from the action momentarily, to bend over to take off my panties, my face was up close and personal with his blue silk boxers. "What the hell, I thought. I'm naked, he may-as-well-be ass out too.

Noticing that very little blood was in any other part of his body, I pulled down his boxers revealing his long, thick, deep chocolate penis.

I don't know what took over me, but after seeing his penis, I dropped to my knees and paid my respects. I had never done that before, but I was so infatuated with Randy, I guess I got beside myself. I was so turned on that I was fantasizing about him asking me to marry him and me saying, "YES! YES!" I'll marry you!

I cupped his tight ass with both hands and took in as much as possible. After a few seconds I looked up and noticed Randy staring me dead in the face with eyes as big as golf balls. He was staring like he was witnessing a murder or something. I stopped immediately.

"You do have protection, right?"

"Yeah," he said as he reached for his wallet that was tucked neatly in the back pocket of his jeans.

As he opened the wrapper to prepare himself, I stood up and got comfortable on the bed. I wanted to turn him on so bad. He was sexy as hell. I mean really sexy! Never trust a big butt and a smile, the old saying goes. Trust me I wanted to fuck his brains out.

I thought back to the time when I was watching one of my fathers' porno tapes, when I was a teenager, and remember seeing a woman that spread her legs as wide as she could showing the inside of her vagina. Her partner was awestruck. I tried that. Just like a stripper, I left nothing to the imagination. I could sense that Randy was nervous. I had him trembling like a little boy who was next in line for a roller coaster ride.

"Well, come on," I said in a whispering seductive voice, as he stood in front of me. He wasn't inside of me two minutes, before he yelled, "Oh God!"

That was the end of that.

That night and the following morning Randy and I didn't say two words to each other. I felt weird. I'm sure he was embarrassed. We started late, but he came early. I had no idea that my aggressive approach was going to end up like that. But, hey, we have today and tomorrow to get it right, I figured. I tried to smile at Randy that morning, but he was having no part of it.

"So what are we going to do today?" I asked.

"I have already made plans," he said dragging around the room collecting his stuff.

"Well, yesterday I told you that we would have the whole weekend alone and you agreed that we would spend it together. What's changed?" I knew the answer; I just wanted to hear what excuse he would give.

"I forgot to tell you that I made other plans. Maybe I'll see you later," he told me as he put on his clothes and walked out.

Since I played myself like booty-licious, I needed to go somewhere and calm down. I decided that I would go to the library. I figured this would give me more time to investigate the lives of the rich and famous...

CHAPTER 11

Distraught about my ordeal with Maxine, I had to do something. After making a collect call to my father's house, I was crossing my fingers, hoping that he wanted to talk to me. When the operator asked, "You have a collect call from Charlene Bedford, will you accept the charges?" I was shocked when he said that he would. I hadn't spoken to my father in months, and I needed him now more than ever.

"Daddy it's me," I said after the operator was off the line.

"How's it going Charlene?" Dad asked.

"It's going okay. I was just calling to apologize," I said with tears in my eyes. "I know that it has been a long time since I spoke with you, but I miss you dad, and I love you."

"I love you too sweetheart," My dad said clearing his throat. "I was so angry when I caught you like that. It has taken me this long to finally forgive you. I want grand kids you know?"

"I know dad. I'm sorry about everything. I'm trying to sort everything out in my head. "

"Where did I go wrong sweetheart?"

"You didn't do anything wrong. I experimented with Stacy, that's all."

"Well, are you back to normal? Straight, I mean?"

"I'm not sure dad. I know that you don't care to hear this, but I felt better with Stacy than with Steven. It felt so natural and she really understands me."

"I would have never guessed that this would have happened to my baby, but if you're sure about this, then I'm going to have to adjust."

"Thanks dad. Is it alright if I come home?"

"I'm looking forward to it."

"I love you daddy."

"I love you too Charlene."

***

When I arrived at my father's house, my dad welcomed me with a hearty embrace. I was happy to be home. After looking around I noticed that my father had done some redecorating. The portrait of my mother that usually hung in the living room was now in the den. The living room furniture had also been rearranged. I walked upstairs to my room with my father following close behind. I was shocked when I saw that my room was exactly the way I left it.

"As I told you on the phone, I have just gotten over what happened here. That's why I haven't come in here to straighten up. Now that you're home, I can let you do it."

"That's fine daddy. It will give me a chance to get reacquainted with the memories," I said.

"It is really good to have you home, Charlene. Maybe later after you are settled, we can go catch a movie and have dinner at your favorite restaurant."

"That would be nice, daddy. I had almost forgotten what a great friend you can be."

Daddy left so I could get my room in order and freshen up for our date. Looking around my room, I remembered all the times I spent in this small space dreaming about what I wanted to do with my life. Now I only wish I could go back in time and just be daddy's little girl.

***

After a weekend of connecting with my roots, I felt much better when I returned to school. Maxine was as cold as ever during the last week of class though. I still managed to earn an "A" in the end.

***

Over the next year or so, I dated a few guys, nothing serious, and eventually put all of my attention on my studies. I was ready to graduate and get on with the rest of my life.

CHAPTER 12

I moved out of my mother's house and was on my own. Mom always said, "Donna, if you make grown up decisions, you have to stand on your own and deal with the consequences." I moved out or should I say I was kicked out due to my little surprise.

***

I was sitting on the window seal of my apartment looking down at the children in their costumes. The kids and their parents were covering the streets on a cold Halloween night. I, along with my other neighbors, threw candy down below to the ones that were looking up at us and yelling, "Trick or treat!"

When I ran out of candy, I started rubbing my very pregnant belly wondering how next year was going to be with my little one. It was just then that I felt an acute pain in my abdomen.

"Calm down little man you still have another month to go," I said as I rubbed my stomach in a circular motion hoping to settle him down.

I doubled over as another sharp pain ripped through me. I knew something was wrong. A parent walking with his little cowboy noticed me in the window and ran with his son in his arms. The man reached the second floor, put his son down, and knocked on the door.

"Daddy, who lives here?" the wide-eyed little boy asked as he looked up at his father, confused.

"I don't know son; the lady in the window looks like she's in trouble." Again the father knocked with just a little more force and urgency.

"Help me," I yelled from behind the door.

"Stand back son, I'm going to have to kick the door down."

The little boy stood against the wall with his hands over his ears. His father kicked the door in and found me on the floor curled up holding my stomach tightly.

"Lady, are you alright?"

"Something's wrong with my baby!"

"My name is Gary and I'm going to help you," he said as he forced the broken door out of the way. He looked around the room and spotted a pillow on the small flowered sofa. Gary ran, got the pillow, and placed it under my head. He took his jacket off and covered me.

"Jay, come inside!" Gary yelled to his son, who was standing outside the door. In the excitement, he forgot about him.

Jay stood in the doorway afraid to move. Gary rushed to the telephone and tried to call 911 for help. All of the lines were tied up.

"Damn it, I can't get through!"

"Do you have a car lady?"

"No. Please do something," I said with a pained look on my face.

Gary ran next door and knocked frantically. An older pray-haired gentleman opened the door and said, "I'm all out of candy. And aren't you a-little-too-old to be trick or treating, sonny?"

Jay stood against the wall with a pale look on his tiny little face; he barely made it out of his father's way.

"Sir, your next door neighbor is in labor and all of the telephone lines are tied up," Gary said with a distressed look on his face.

"You mean Miss Donna is having her baby? But it ain't time yet. I'll pull my car around the front and you get Miss Donna," the old man said as he grabbed his coat and keys and headed downstairs.

Gary rushed back to my side and helped me to my feet. He draped his coat around my shoulders and we headed out the door slowly. Jay came to my side and tried to help like his father was doing. I forced Jay a slight smile through the pain. When we reached downstairs, I saw Mr. Waterman waiting with the car door opened. Jay got in the front with Mr. Waterman and Gary got in the back seat with me. Off we went to Memorial hospital, five blocks from my apartment. I screamed and panted all the way there.

When I got to the hospital, I was introduced to my team of nurses. The RN was Mrs. Sandra Turner and the LPN was Ms. Vernese Knight. I was in so much pain that I could only nod solemnly in response to the introduction. As the nurse adjusted the pillow under my head, she asked, "Are you okay sweetheart? Is there anything I else I can do for you?"

"I don't want to go through this alone," I stated. "I wished that he was here," I cried.

"Who are you talking about? Is there someone I need to call?" Vernese asked.

"Yes, his name is Gregory Turner and he can be reached at 252-4228." Just as Vernese goes to place the call, my water breaks...

***

After an intense delivery, I was holding my beautiful baby boy. He was 7lbs and 9oz. As nurse Knight walked back into the room, I asked, "Were you able to get in touch with Gregory?"

"I left a message with his secretary who ensured me she would give him the message."

"Well, I sure hope Diane gives him the message, because she never gives him my messages."

"She assured me that she would give Mr. Turner the message," Vernese replied.

As Nurse Turner enters the room she looks at the baby and then at Donna and asks, "Who did you say the father was?"

"Gregory Turner," Donna responded.

"What a coincidence. My husband's name is Gregory Turner," Nurse Turner stated with a puzzled look...

CHAPTER 13

I decided to go to the library, looking for the ingredient that seemed to be the key to becoming rich. *Someday, the name Tanya Brown would be among the list of millionaires,* I thought to myself.

I spent about three hours looking up information on some of the wealthiest people in the world. To my amazement, I found out that Bill Gates attended Harvard but did not graduate, Heather Locklear attended UCLA but left school during her junior year to pursue an acting career, and P. Diddy dropped out of Howard University before starting his record label. Furthermore, Chris Rock and D.L. Hughley never graduated from high school, and actor Charles Dutton had served time in prison before getting his big break. I researched even further and found out that Demi Moore was also a high school dropout.

I was now more confused than ever. I was certain that I needed a college degree to become rich, but it didn't appear to be the answer for some of the wealthiest people in the world. I walked out of the library with many ideas running around in my head. Finally, it hit me! All of these individuals pursued careers that had wealth potential. Wow! A simple concept, but many people never consider it. Education is necessary for however long it takes to realize where you will make your money. If you want to be rich through a college education, your field of study must be one where the highest level of success will bring you millions. Degrees in the following fields are a good start towards attaining wealth: political science, acting/theater, engineering, broadcast journalism, movie-video-film, computer technology, or business. However, you don't have to graduate to become wealthy. Many people get a job out of high school or college that at the highest level of success, millions are not the payoff. The best high school teachers, military soldiers, law enforcement officers, or social workers will never be rich if that is their only income stream, no matter how many awards or promotions they receive. Singers, models, athletes, real estate brokers, investment specialists, business owners, actors, doctors, authors, news anchors, lawyers... are the only way to go. Unless, of course, you are going to invest most of your money from a low-wage-paying profession in your younger days, and enjoy your millions as a senior citizen. In the long run though, in any career, it's not how much you make, it's how much you save and invest. I got it!

"Mom," I said after calling home.

"Hi Tanya, how's my baby doing?"

"I'm doing fine mama. I have been doing research on some of the wealthiest people in the world."

"Yeah. What did you come up with?"

"I'm going to open my own business mama."

"What type of business Tanya?"

"I want to open my own public speaking firm."

"That sounds like you."

"Thanks mom. I realize that I have to be good at something. Something I love that pays a lot of money. Motivational speaking will do that."

"Have you figured out where you want to open your business?"

"I'm not sure. I know I want to do an internship somewhere this summer. Hopefully, I'll learn even more."

***

I decided to go to the student center and look on the bulletin board for internships. I found the perfect one located in Savannah, Georgia. The letter read, "Keith "Preacher" Brown the Motivator of the Millennium, was looking for an aspiring motivational speaker to do an internship with his company. He was also the author of the award winning book "CHITLINS" (Creative, Helpful, Intuitive, Thoughts, Lifting, Individuals, Naturally, Seeking). I called his office and spoke to his secretary.

"Mr. Brown is out of the office right now, perhaps someone else here can help you?" the person on the other end responded.

"My name is Tanya Brown and I wanted to apply for the internship position. What is your name and what do you do for Mr. Brown."

"My name is Rosa, and I am his personal assistant."

She asked me a few questions, and sounded as though she was happy with my answers. "I'll be sure to tell Mr. Brown that I think you would be perfect for the position."

"Thank," I said.

"I'll have him call you as soon as he gets in," she assured me.

About twenty-five minutes after my phone conversation with Rosa, the phone rang. "May I speak to Ms. Brown Please," The male voice asked.

"This is she," I responded.

"This is Keith Brown. You have obviously left a lasting impression on my secretary. Rosa is a good judge of character and if you are good enough for her, than you are certainly good enough for me."

He filled me in on the dates and expectations, and I gladly accepted. Two months later, I found myself on a plane headed to beautiful Savannah, Georgia to learn from the "Motivator of the Millennium."

When I arrived in Savannah, I was greeted with a limousine that had a full schedule of sight seeing before I had the chance to meet Mr. Brown. He was not only paying for all of my expense, he included a stipend in the amount of five hundred dollars, for my time. And Although I found it quite strange initially, Mr. Brown bought me a ticket to the Lil' Romeo concert that was being held in the Savannah Civic. I was a fan of Master P but never in a million years would I have guessed that I would be a fan of his son, Lil Romeo. The boy is bad. Lil' Romeo put on an awesome show!

Mr. Brown was a personal friend of Master P's, so I was able to go back stage and meet the millionaire and his son. That was a night I will never forget.

After slobbering all over Master P, I was escorted back to my Limo and driven to Semolina's restaurant. Mr. Brown was there waiting for me. He let me know that he would be speaking at Beach High School on the following morning and that he wanted me to go with him. I was staying at the Country Inn & Suites. When I got back to my room, I went straight to bed and awaited my 8:00 a.m. wake-up call.

In the morning I immediately got dressed and remained in the lobby for Mr. Brown to pick me up and take me to the school. When we got to the school, I was introduced to the principal and many of the faculty before taking my seat.

If you have never had the opportunity to hear Mr. Keith "Preacher" Brown give one of his awe-inspiring messages, I'm here to tell you, "You are missing out on a life changing experience. The man is Awesome!" I, along with everyone else, was captivated by his inspirational message. At the conclusion of his uplifting message, not only did he receive a standing ovation from the crowd, but everyone was asking, "How soon can you come back?"

I left that school auditorium on cloud nine. Mr. Brown had ignited my soul! When we returned to his office later that day, I had the privilege of watching a clip of Mr. Brown on the Apollo with Steve Harvey. Again, he dazzled the audience and received a standing ovation. Now looking back on it, what impressed me the most about Mr. Brown was that his messages were never the same. He has the awesome ability to dazzle any audience. I can still remember the teachers at the last school that I had the privilege of hearing him speak at saying, "You Go Boy," after he delivered another one of his powerful messages....

CHAPTER 14

I was having a blast in Savannah! Mr. Brown had arranged for me to be taken to downtown historic district. I was taken to River Street. My escort,Dave Williams and I, enjoyed the wonderful southern music and the cool breeze resonating from the river. As I walked along River Street, I was taking in the sites and sounds of one of the most beautiful small towns in the world. There were musicians along the sidewalk and vocalists in the taverns. Free entertainment had never been better. I did, however, manage to pull myself away from all of the excitement, to call home.

"Hello."

"Hey, Mom, it's Tanya."

"Are you still in Savannah?"

"Sure am. I've got a week to go," I said.

"Have you talked to Donna lately?"

"No. I haven't talked to her in over a year. Her mother's number has been changed and it is unlisted."

"Well, I saw her at the post office today. Let me give you her new number," Mom said while I wrote the number down. Mom and I talked briefly, but I was eager to hear from Donna.

"What's up girl?" I asked after calling Donna's apartment.

"A lot," Donna said. "I have had a baby by a married man, my mother kicked me out, and I am holding down two jobs."

"Shit! You have been through a lot."

"I guess you can say that. Mom and I are speaking again so that's the only good thing," Donna said. "I've got more bad news to tell you though."

"What happened?"

"My mother called me earlier and told me that Julian was in the paper for raping some girl."

"What, My Julian?" I said in shock.

"Yeah, girl," Donna said.

"No way. Hell, he didn't even try to have sex with me in high school, and I probably would have given him some. It must be a mistake."

"I know girl. It must be."

"The last time I heard from him, he had one class to take before graduating with a B.A. in Psychology. He had been taking a full load each quarter to include summer school and was scheduled to graduate a full year early. He was to begin working on his masters immediately following graduation. I don't know what's going on. Donna, please find out and call me back. I thought the unforgettable storm was behind us, but for Julian's family, I see it's starting all over again."

"Okay. I heard that he's in the county jail. I will go down there right now, and I'll call you when I find out something."

"I'll be in my hotel room waiting on your call. The number is (912) 651-3502, room 125."

"I'll fill you in when I get back."

"Bye Girl."

"Bye Tanya."

When I made it back to my hotel room, I thought long and hard about Julian. *How could this be happening? Julian was the perfect gentleman. What could have gone wrong?* I thought about all of the things he and I had ever done together and all of his talents. He was an excellent swimmer, a good student, and even sang at weddings.

He had recently received an award from the big-brothers program, for the excellent job he had done mentoring and tutoring young students over the years. Even after high school, he was still giving back to students in the community. Just as I started into my next half-hour of contemplation, the phone rang.

"Tanya?"

"Yeah. What did you find out?"

"It's a real mess girl. The damn girl that he was accused of raping told him that she was eighteen, turns out that she is only fifteen. She had a fake I.D. and everything. He was arrested for statutory rape."

"Shit! That little bitch! I knew something was up. How can he be charged with anything if that's the case?"

"Well as of right now, they haven't found her fake I.D."

"That bitch needs to be put under the jail." Damn! Damn! Damn! How could this shit be happening? Julian is a good person. Now he will have a record, and it could possibly mess up the rest of his life. God Damn that little bitch!"

"Julian's court date is on the 28th according to the paper," Donna said, now looking at her calendar. "Hell that is only two days away. Hopefully, it will all work out."

"I wasn't scheduled to leave until tomorrow, but tell Julian I'm on my way."

"Enough of the bad news how was your internship?" Donna asked.

"This internship has been fantastic. All of my expenses were paid for and everything. I made a couple of dollars so I can afford to pay the difference for a flight out tonight. Can you pick me up at the airport?"

"Sure. Just call me on my cell when you get your flight arrangements. I'll go back down to the jail real quick to let Julian know that you are on your way."

"Thanks girl. Let me get ready. I'll call you when I get to the airport."

"You do that."

CHAPTER 15

There were no flights from Savannah to New York so I had to catch a connecting flight in Atlanta. When I arrived at the Atlanta airport, I was really down in the dumps about what was happening to Julian. To add insult to injury, my flight had been canceled. While I waited around to see if there were any other flights on another airline, I started a conversation with a young lady who was scheduled to be on the flight with me. She was a very pretty girl, yet saying some very ugly things. As I excused myself to use the restroom, I ran into Charlene. She was wearing a neat maroon summer dress and brown sandals.

Coincidentally, she was supposed to be on the same flight with me. "So how have you been girl?" Charlene asked.

"I'm doing fine."

"Damn! I needed to be in New York tonight," Charlene said frantically after I told her about the flight cancellation.

"I know what you mean. I was hoping to get back tonight myself."

"I don't know if you remember Kelly Blackburn?"

"No. That name doesn't ring a bell."

"Well, anyway, she's getting married tomorrow, and I've already missed the damn rehearsal dinner."

"Sorry to hear that. I'm trying to get home to see one of my friends too," I said not mentioning Julian's name intentionally.

"You know what?"

"What?" I replied.

"I was so caught up in this plane shit; I didn't realize how attractive you've become. You're very attractive Tanya."

"Well, thank you."

"No. I mean really attractive."

I raised an eyebrow, "Come again."

"Has anyone ever told you that you look like Serena Williams? You've got the beautifully sculpted body and everything."

I have been complimented on my body, but you are the first to tell me that I look like Serena Williams."

"Well you do."

"Hey, weren't you two ladies on the flight to New York?" a white heavy-set lady approached us and asked.

"Yes," Charlene retorted.

"There are no more flights to New York tonight on any airlines. You need to go back to the ticket counter to pick up the vouchers to get your free hotel rooms."

"Thanks," I responded.

After getting our hotel vouchers Charlene asked, "Hey, would you like to get something to eat?"

"Yeah," I said as Charlene and I promenaded to a Chili's bar in the Airport. As we sat down, we continued our conversation. Charlene looked over the menu and gazed over at me.

"How many grooms and brides maids?"

"Eight of each. They have been together eight years now, and I'm sorry the-

"Can I take your order?" The bartender interrupted.

"Do you know what you want?" Charlene asked seductively.

"Can I have a minute?"

"I'll come back."

"Can I ask you something, Tanya?"

"Yeah," I responded.

"Are you involved with anyone right now?"

"No. Why do you ask," I said.

"I dated a lady for two months, but we broke up about a year ago. I haven't had a serious relationship since."

"Oh," I said surprised. "How long have you dated women?"

"I came out about a year after you saw me with Darryl."

"Have you dated any men since then?"

"Yes. I dated two in college. Men just weren't doing it for me."

"Well, I know that little dick Darryl wasn't doing much for you."

We laughed.

"So, what is it about women that you like so much?" I asked.

"Their scent, their gentle touch, the way their clothes caress their body. Just everything," Charlene replied.

"I glanced at Charlene with intrigue. The bartender returned. "Are you ready to order?"

"I'll have fajitas," I said.

"I was going to order the same thing; why don't we just get fajitas for two?"

"Okay," I said with a girlish grin.

As we enjoyed our meal and talked over a drink or two, we noticed that the establishment was closing. "We need to find out where the hotel is," Charlene suggested. We handed the bartender our vouchers and headed out. Charlene made it a point to walk in front of me so that I could enjoy the rear view of her flawless body. I admired her just as I did when we were teenagers. *Damn she looks good in her clothes. I wonder if she still looks as good out of them*, I pondered. Charlene caught me admiring her out of the corner of her eye, and I quickly looked away. When we got outside of the airport and flagged down a cab, I reached for the handle on the door.

"I got it," Charlene said.

I was enjoying the seduction. My head was saying yes to her seduction, but my mouth couldn't part with the words. When we got to the hotel, Embassy Suites, Charlene backed off.

"Are you together?" the attendant asked.

"Not really," Charlene said quickly.

"The reason I asked is because we only have one room available, but it does have double beds."

"That's fine with me. I would love to share a room with her," I responded.

"Well if it's okay with her, it's definitely okay with me," Charlene said.

When we made it to our room I told Charlene that I needed to call my mother and tell her that I would be there in the morning. Charlene told me that was fine before, grabbing a few items out of her suitcase and dashing to the shower.

When she returned, she was wearing silk navy shorts and a white T-shirt. "Is everything okay?" Charlene asked.

"Yes. Thanks for asking." *Wow! Her legs are still as toned as they were in high school*, I thought.

"It's kind of warm in here, is it okay if I turn on the air conditioner?" Charlene asked.

"Sure" I said as I admired her erect nipples pressing against her T-shirt. Every time Charlene moved, I became more curious. As she turned the air on, she said, "I need to put on some lotion."

After locating my bottle of lotion, "Catch, you can borrow mine," I said as I tossed her the container.

Charlene applied lotion to every curve of her legs. She sensually massaged her legs and outer thighs. I nearly lost my composure when she applied lotion to her inner thighs.

"Can you put some on my back?" Charlene asked as she sat down on the bed.

"Sure," I said as I got up and nervously sat next to her. I assisted in lifting her T-shirt to reveal her back. As I applied the lotion to her back, she and I inhaled the sweet scent of passion fruit. I became aroused. I moved my hands from her back to her arms and I gently brushed against her erect nipples before moving down to her stomach. Charlene's body exhaled. Charlene put her hands on top of mine. She embraced my hands and pulled them up to her nipples. I tensed. She caressed my hands to help relax me. Charlene lifted her head back and whispered, "Come here," as she pulled me around to face her.

"You are very sexy Tanya," Charlene said.

I tensed up again. "Thanks," I replied. Then she pulled me closer. I exhaled.

Charlene kissed me on my lips.

"I'm going to take a quick shower. I'll be right back," I said as I grabbed a fresh set of panties, matching bra, and my White Diamond perfume.

After getting undressed, I jumped in the shower. I thought back to that day when I saw Charlene in the woods. My childhood fantasy was only moments away. As I washed myself, one side of me kept saying, no way. Yet, the beads of water pulsating my nipples and the throbbing sensation that ignited in between my legs, indicated otherwise.

After turning the water off, I pulled the white shower curtain back. I grabbed a fluffy white towel, stepped on the floor mat, and enjoyed a chilling sensation that would not leave my body. I put on my black satin panties and bra, and sprayed my White Diamond on my hands and rubbed them on my body.

"Damn, you smell good!" Charlene said excitingly as I entered the room. "That's why I love women; clean and sexy. And if I need to be fucked, we can strap it on, HIV and pregnancy free."

"You are wild."

"No. Just keeping it real. Can you stand in the middle of the room for a second?"

"Sure. What's up?"

"You'll see."

Charlene turned on every light in the room and took off her shorts. To my surprise, she was not wearing any panties. I had seen her naked before, but tonight she looked more mind-blowing than ever. She leisurely walked over to the small burgundy couch and placed her shorts there. She pulled her T-shirt over her head, put it on top of her shorts, and sauntered towards me. Within five seconds, she was standing naked in front of me. She was wearing blue eye shadow and bright red lipstick. Although her breasts were large, they were the most perfect set of breast I had ever seen, still perky, with no droop.

Charlene dropped to her knees right in front of me, and reached for my panties.

I didn't stop her.

After taking my panties off, she put the palms of her hands in between my legs and spread my legs apart. I stood motionless in the middle of the room. Charlene, on her knees, centered herself in between my legs. She moved from her butt touching her heels to a perfect ninety-degree angle. She arched her head back and ran her fingers through her silky sandy brown hair, revealing her beautiful face. Her lips and then her tongue engaged me. I leaned my head back and closed my eyes. I let out a sigh of pure delight. She licked and kissed me like never before. As she engaged me, she sensually ran her perfectly manicured red nails across my ass. I began to quiver. She racked her nails slowly, all the way down to my ankles. It was pure ecstasy. As she tasted my wetness, I wanted more. I took off my bra and began caressing my breast and pinching my nipples. I was on fire. As I moaned, Charlene became more aggressive. She pushed her tongue as far as she could inside of me. I couldn't take it any more. My knees were so weak that I was about to crumble. I took a step back, grabbed Charlene by her hands, and pulled her to her feet and then to the bed. I let one hand go as I pushed my suitcase still open, to the floor.

As my clothes leaped out of my suitcase, I whispered in Charlene's ear, "I want you to fuck me," as I lay on my back at the edge of the bed.

On the burgundy colored bed spread, Charlene rolled me onto my stomach. She went to retrieve her treat, and strapped it on. When she returned, she spread my legs slightly and started teasing me with that awesome tongue of hers. Boy did she know how to make me shiver. She reached under my midsection with both hands and pulled me toward her. As I reached the doggy style position, my pussy made a popping sound which I took to mean, open for business.

As her treat entered me, it felt as natural as any man I had ever had. As she thrusted, I moaned with shear delight. She was hitting all the right places, especially my "G" spot. She was really working it, or should I say, working me. She would go midway and then all the way. She was a real pro at using that treat. My hands were filled with the bed spread. As she thrusted, I clinched tighter.

After countless thrusts of pleasure I pleaded, "Let me turn over."

This woman was making me feel so good that I wanted to touch her. After I turned over and got comfortable, she entered me again. I pulled my knees as far back as I could so that the treat could go as deep as possible. I pushed the hair away from her face and kissed her. Her tongue was incredible. Wherever I wanted to meet her tongue, it was already there waiting. Our chemistry was like no other chemistry I had ever encountered. As she thrusted, her breast rubbed against mine. Her bright red nipples were erect and tantalizing. Charlene was so incredibly beautiful. I kissed her breasts, her lips, and again I enjoyed her tongue. She made love to me like no man had ever done before. As we started to perspire profusely, she collapsed in my arms. We were both extremely tired yet very much fulfilled.

I looked over at Charlene who was now fast asleep. Although I was worn out and feeling shamefaced, I knew that I would do it all over again in the morning if she wanted to. And although I had fun, this was one skeleton that I felt would truly be left in the closet.

Our flight was scheduled for nine a.m., so I set the alarm clock for seven. I called mom and Donna and gave them my itinerary.

CHAPTER 16

The next morning while on the plane, Charlene and I exchanged numbers. It was a good thing that we were not sitting next to each other on the plane. There was no telling what we might have done.

When we de-boarded, while standing in the tunnel leading from the plane to the airport, we hugged and vowed to stay in touch. Charlene looked deep into my eyes, licked her lips, and began to lean towards me.

I then said quickly, I'll be in touch," and turned and continued through the tunnel.

My life had really been turned upside down, in a matter of a couple of hours. When I exited the tunnel, my mom, Donna, and her son Jarrell were there waiting for me.

"Hey girl, how was your trip?" Donna asked.

"It... It... It... was okay," I responded.

"Are you okay?"

"I'm fine. A long night, that's all," I said after kissing Jarrell on the forehead.

"Isn't that Charlene Bedford I see coming up behind you?"

"Where? I don't see her."

"Right there silly."

"Oh that is Charlene, isn't it," I said trying to sound credible.

"Hey Charlene, long time no see girl. I didn't know you were on the same flight with me," I said.

Charlene had a perplexed look on her face.

"You remember my mom and Donna don't you?" I asked knowing damn well that she did.

"Whatever Tanya, she said under her breath. "Hey, how's everybody doing?"

"Good to see you Charlene," my mother said after a warm embrace.

As I walked to the conveyor and retrieved my luggage, I was ashamed of myself, and nervous as hell. I didn't know whether Charlene was going to tell my mom or Donna what we did, so I glanced over at Charlene, put my index finger over my mouth and removed it quickly to let her know not to blow my cover. Charlene frowned, shook her head in disbelief and walked away.

As I got into the car and left the airport, I felt somewhat relieved. Mom took Donna home and Donna agreed to pick me up in the morning to take me to the jail.

CHAPTER 17

Once I got home, mom could tell that something was bothering me. Luckily, I had Julian's situation to divert her attention.

"You don't look so good baby."

"I know. It's just that Julian being locked up, really has me down."

"I know baby. It will be alright. I'm just happy to have you home. Does your father know you're here?"

"No. I haven't had a chance to call him yet. I'll be here for a couple of days. I'm sure that I will call him before I go back."

When I made it to my room, it was just the way I left it on my last visit home. I took a shower thinking about Charlene, and immediately went to bed.

***

In the morning, I stood at my window and watched clouds pass through the sky. The sun appeared in the blue sky between three billowing clouds and glistened on the still-wet grass.

I wondered what Charlene was doing, what she was thinking. I had wanted her so much last night! Even now, I could feel the heat from our affair reverberating through my body. Am I a lesbian? Was I falling in love with her? Do I still desire men? I decided to take a cold shower.

The phone rang.

"Tanya?"

"Good morning, Donna," I replied.

"I'll be over shortly."

"I'll be ready," I said as I hung the telephone up on my way to the shower.

When Donna arrived, I couldn't take it anymore. I had to tell somebody, and Donna, of course, was my best friend. I didn't know exactly how to tell her seeing that I didn't want her to think that I was coming-on-to-her or anything. I came up with an idea.

"I have been meaning to ask you something."

"What's that, Tanya?"

"I have been reading a ton of books lately and many of them are talking about gay and lesbian relationships. Why is that?"

"What authors are you talking about exactly?"

"E. Lynn Harris, Eric Jerome Dickey, you know, the big time authors."

"Heck, beats me. I was kinda wondering that myself. I think they are trying to address the fact that there are more gays and lesbians then people think. Many of them are in the closet. What do you think?"

"Um, Um I don't know, I guess I see it the way you do, I...I guess," I said nervously.

"Have you ever thought about being with another woman?" Donna asked.

"Hell no!" I said trying to sound convincing. "Have you?"

"Well mom said that it was normal for people to be curious about anything that is highly publicized. You know, like drinking and smoking."

"Yeah, I guess so. But you still haven't answered my question."

"What question was that?"

"Have you ever thought about being with a woman?"

"Not really. I mean, I am curious to what all of the fuss is about, but I am quite content with men."

"Are you sure?"

"Damn girl, you're asking me like maybe you're not sure. What's gotten into you?"

"Nothing, I was just asking. You know, all the books we're reading and all."

"Well, seeing that this has really stumped you, I'll call in sick today and, we can go by and talk to my mom about it when we leave the jail?"

"Oh, I don't know about that."

"Girl my mom is cool. You know that. She will talk about anything with anybody. She taught sociology and psychology in college. She has an answer for any and everything that deals with the behavior of people. She can go on for hours. You won't have to say a word. I'll ask all of the questions, how's that?"

"Cool."

CHAPTER 18

When we made it to the jail, we had to fill out all sorts of paperwork. Julian had received a lot of support from his church members, and they had been there to pray with him every night. It had been five days, and I was sure that this jail thing was taking a toll on him. He had never been in trouble before. Heck, he had never served a day in detention in high school. I felt so sorry for him.

After finishing the paperwork and showing my I.D., I was escorted to the visiting room and told that it would be a few minutes. When Julian arrived, he was as clean as a whistle. He had shaved his head bald and removed all facial hair. When he entered the room, I hugged him and said, "I'm so sorry Julian. If there is anything I can do, just let me know."

"Your being here is enough. Thanks for coming."

"You will always be one of my best friends, and I will always be in your corner. You know that, right?"

"Well, if you could come under these circumstances, if I had any doubt, I don't anymore."

"What made you decide to shave your hair off?"

"When Donna told me that you were coming, I wanted to clean up a bit."

"Well, you clean up very well, looking like Michael Jordan or somebody," I said sarcastically.

We laughed.

"Well, I know you want to know everything, so I am going to start from the beginning. Do you remember Lolita Davis?"

"No. Refresh my memory."

"She was in the eighth grade at the time, but she filled out early. We used to call her boom-boom."

"Oh. You're talking about Lu-Lu. Ya'll nick-named her that because she had big breasts and a big butt."

"That's right. The young girl that I am accused of raping was built just like boom-boom. The little bitch, excuse my language, showed me a fake I.D. and everything. I told you that already haven't I?"

"No, but Donna did. Have they found the I.D. yet?"

"Not yet."

"It's hard to believe this is happening."

"I know. Get this, When I showed up for my arraignment, her fucking lawyer had her dressed in a black and white schoolgirl uniform and black and white saddle oxfords. To top that shit off, she was wearing her hair in two ponytails. I really did look like Chester the Molester."

"So what happens next?"

"My lawyer is basically going to every place in New York that makes fake I.D.'s and seeing if he can find the place that made hers."

What is he expecting to find?" Donna asked.

"Well, according to my lawyer, These I.D. places usually make several copies of each fake I.D. Youngsters usually misplace them or have them confiscated and are in need of another one. These I.D. places will normally provide them with another one at full price."

"If he doesn't find this place, what will happen then?" Donna asked.

"Well that's the basis for my case. If he doesn't find the place, I guess I'll be getting raped in prison. I don't mean to keep harping on it ya'll, but that little bitch was saying shit like, you wanna get a room and everything. I would have never guessed that she was only fifteen."

"Well, if your lawyer is worth shit, he'll find out where her I.D. was made, and this nightmare will soon be over. You have believed in God up until now, so don't stop believing when your faith is challenged."

"Preach sister, preach," he said.

We laughed.

"Well, I know you ladies have some catching up to do yourselves. So thanks again for coming. I need to go to my cell and jot down everything that I remember about that little bitch. Maybe I'll think of something that will help my case."

"Well, I'll be in town for a few more days. I will be at the courthouse on Wednesday."

"Thanks for the support ladies. I'll see you there," Julian said as we departed.

Turmoil in July. I was trying to figure out my sexuality, Julian was trying to figure out his fate. We were joined at the hip when we were younger and now our hips have gotten us where we are today. I didn't know how to express what I was feeling for Charlene, because I knew that it was taboo in the eyes of those around me. I truly enjoyed my sexual experience, yet I felt too ashamed and embarrassed to tell anyone about it. I was on my way to see Donna's mom and hopefully she had some answers for me.

CHAPTER 19

As I entered the Short's residence, I was a little uneasy. But after sitting down on the sofa, I was able to relax a little while I waited for Ms. Short to appear. As she entered the room I said, "Hi Ms. Short, how are you?"

"I'm fine Tanya. Haven't seen you in a long, long time. You look good though. What are you doing now? Where are you living and all that?"

"Well, I'm going back to school in a couple of weeks to finish my senior year at the University of Miami."

"What are you majoring in?"

"Business, I want to open my own public speaking company."

"That sounds good. Who is going to be your audience?"

"I figured I would start in elementary schools, and work my way up to colleges. I want to teach them how to improve their grades. I've learned a number of techniques since I've been in college, and I want to integrate those techniques with the motivational speeches that I have been writing for years."

"Sounds like you got it all figured out."

"Mom?"

"Yes, Donna?"

"We had a couple of questions that we would like for you to answer."

"Well, if I know the answer, I will certainly tell you."

"Tanya and I have been reading a lot of books lately and the books keep addressing lesbian and gay relationships. We just wanted to know what your thoughts were on gay and lesbian relationships."

"Oh, a simple question with a simple answer. I taught sociology over at the college as both of you know. That topic came up often, along with racism and sexism. One thing that I taught my students was; all behaviors are learned. Heterosexuality included. Typically, what happens is that good or bad experiences with regard to sexuality determine whether you will be straight or gay. For example, if you are a young girl who has been raped by an uncle, father, or grandfather, you will view sex and men totally different from someone who had not endured the same. Sociological statistics show a disproportionate number of women who have become prostitutes, were raped by family members. Meaning, today, many of them don't equate sex with love. They have been stripped of their desire to love a man and seek a female for understanding and companionship. So prostitutes, while having sex with men, truly see sex as a way to make money. It's a job to them, not an emotional attachment."

"Wow! that's deep," I said.

"Oh it gets better. Most men on the other hand, want sex all the time. If they are constantly being rejected by women it still doesn't change the fact that they want sex. Homosexuals statistically have sex ten times more than heterosexuals. What does that tell you?"

"Men are horny as hell?" We laughed.

"You got it. Homosexual, heterosexual it doesn't matter. A man is a man when it comes to sex. Most of the homosexual literature that I read over the years clearly shows that after several failed attempts to attract women, some men adopt the theory known as the Path of Least Resistance. They will accept oral and anal sex from whoever is willing to give it."

"That's crazy mom. Are you saying that women are to blame for gay men?"

"No. I'm not. It is still ultimately up to the man to stay strong, so to speak, until the right woman comes along. But I do, however, know that women contribute to it. I hear the same things you hear. Women boasting that they don't need a man. So what does the man eventually start saying?"

"I don't need a woman," Donna said.

"That's right. If women are not open to exploring relationships with men, then men will have to look elsewhere. Wouldn't you agree?"

"Yeah, I guess so, if you put it like that," I said.

"An easier example for you to digest would be men in prison. Statistically, the number of homosexuals in prison has quadrupled over the last ten years. Studies show that some men are known as the women in the prison, if you can imagine that. I studied and viewed a number of documentaries and read countless articles that showed the feminine male being lead around by the so-called masculine one. The trade-off for having sex with one prison bully was protection from the others. They obviously realized that women were out of the picture all together, when given a life sentence, so if they were to have any type of sex, it could only be with another man. Any more questions?"

"Well, you haven't said as much about lesbians as you have about gays, Ms. Short."

"You're right. I'll address that now. Over the past twenty-five years, dozens of sociologists, anthropologists, and psychologists have studied lesbian relationships. What the studies show is that most lesbian relationships' last between two and four years. Not only that, most lesbians don't stay with their first, second, or third lover. What does that tell you?"

"It sounds like they are just as horny and confused as heterosexuals, mama."

"In a way, you're right. Sex in many of these relationships, is the number one thing in the beginning and just like with heterosexual relationships, if that's the primary focus, the relationship won't last. "

"Why aren't more women lesbians?"

"What do you mean?"

"Because most of the girls I know do plenty of male-bashing," I added.

"Everybody's experience is different. Some women who are male-bashing might only be talking about one bad relationship. As long as there have been good relationships that they can draw from, they will always have a desire for men and are less likely to be a dyke. I have had pleasant experiences with men so I chose to be with them. I love the way they think, look, smell, and feel. If perhaps I was molested as a child, beat up by my boyfriends, and never seemed to have a happy, healthy, relationship with a man, I would have learned that they weren't right for me. Not to say that I would be a lesbian, but I probably wouldn't want to have anything to do with a man. Now, who really wanted to know the answers to these questions?"

"I did Ms. Short," I said cowardly.

"I see." Ms. Short paused. "Donna, could you go to the store and pick up some flounder for dinner."

"Sure mom."

"I need to talk to Tanya for a few minutes, hear?"

"Okay mama, I shouldn't be gone long."

"Now where were we? You see, Donna made a grown up decision when she got pregnant with Jarrell, so I had to put her out."

"Why did you put her out if you don't mind me asking?"

"I told Donna that if she ever got pregnant, she would have to stand on her own two feet. She knew how to lie down like adults do, so it was time for her to hit the clock like we do," she added.

"I see," I said.

"Now where were we? Oh, yeah. Does your mother know?"

"Know what?"

"Tanya I've been around a long time, that's why I asked Donna to leave. You have it written all over your face, honey. Now what is said here will stay right here. If you want to tell anyone, that is your business, but you have my word, I won't tell a soul."

"If I were a lesbian why should I trust you?"

"I'm going to tell you something that I never told any of my students. This will help you to live with your sexuality without shame or embarrassment."

"I'm listening."

"All men are homosexuals and all women are lesbians."

"Say what?"

"I'll start with the men. Statistics show that 99% of all men masturbate. What does that tell you?"

"I'm not sure I'm following you."

"I'll tell it to you straight then. When a man jacks-off, is it a man's hand or a woman's hand that jacks him off?"

"It's his hand."

The operative word, "His." So if a man says that he can't be sexually aroused by the touch of a man, you know statistically speaking, he is a God Damn liar! Would you agree?"

"Wow! Donna was right, you do know everything."

"I wouldn't say all of that, but the same applies to women. Women use sex toys, rub themselves do whatever they have to in order to have an orgasm. Where are the men when these women are stimulating themselves?"

"Obviously not there. Thanks for clearing that up. That was deep."

"Does your mother know that you have feeling for another woman?"

"No."

"Well, as I said earlier, your secret is safe with me. I have been teaching for over thirty years, and I have seen young men and women commit suicide over this very issue. If I were to tell your secret, I would be responsible for anything that happens to you. You are like one of my own. I wouldn't tell anybody anything unless you wanted me to."

"Thanks, I appreciate that," I said.

"Now the flipside of this conversation: Don't define yourself by your sexual orientation, either."

"What do you mean by that?" I asked.

"If you were truly a lesbian you would be attracted to all women. Are you equally attracted to all women?"

"No."

"Exactly, so don't define yourself by your sexual orientation. We fall in love with individuals not a vagina or a penis. When you found yourself attracted to people when you were in school, I'm pretty sure that you didn't have to see what was between their legs before you became interested in them. Am I right?"

"Yes Ma'am."

"If heterosexuals were truly heterosexual, is that for twenty-four hours a day, seven days a week?"

"It should be, I suppose."

"Well, what sexual orientation does a woman have when she tells her mate that she's not in the mood?"

"I don't know."

"My point exactly. Nobody knows why we want sex sometimes and sometimes we don't. Again, that is why I say, you can't logically define yourself merely by sexual orientation."

"Ms. Short, you are brilliant."

"Well, thank you," she said as she stood up to take a bow. "Now why don't you tell me about this woman that you apparently have feelings for?"

"It was so weird. I had a rendezvous with an old high school friend and, I can't seem to get her out of my head?"

"Does she still live here?"

"Yes and no. Her father still lives here but she's a student in Atlanta. She was in town, from what I can remember, for just a couple of days.

"Well, where did you see her?" Ms. Short asked.

"Actually, it happened the night that I was on my way here. I saw her in the airport. We talked about old times and one thing led to another."

"Do you have a number for her?"

"Yes ma'am," I said.

"Why don't you call her?"

"I'm not sure if she still wants to be involved with me," I said as I began to cry.

"Call her. That's the only way that you will know for sure."

"May I use your phone?" I said as I wiped the tears from my eyes.

"Sure darling, go right ahead."

As I continued drying my face, I thumbed through my pocketbook to find Charlene's number. I was scared as hell because the last thing I needed to hear was that she moved on. I missed her dearly. I thought back to that night and I felt like I needed her now, more than ever. The image of her lying next to me kept flashing through my mind. I had my chance at the airport but I was too ashamed to go after her then. I'm hoping that she still wants me now. After feverishly looking for her number, I found it.

"Hello."

"Charlene?"

"This is she."

"This is Tanya, how's it going?"

"Who?"

"Tanya," I said now feeling forgotten.

"Tanya, I was hoping that you would call me. I am in the car, and I traveled through a dead spot and could barely hear you. How are you doing girl?"

"Okay I guess. I was thinking about you," I said.

"Well, why don't we get together tonight. You are still in New York aren't you?"

"Yes!" I said with excitemeht in my voice.

"Where do you want to meet?"

"I don't care. Have you had dinner yet?"

"No."

"My dad let me drive one of his cars. Where are you? I can come and pick you up."

"How about meeting me at the Walgreens on the south side?" I suggested.

"Okay. I'm about ten minutes from there."

"Well, I'll meet you there in ten minutes," I said and hung up the phone.

"Ms. Short----

"That's okay baby. I'll tell Donna something came up. Run along now and have yourself a good time!"

"Thanks, Ms Short. Thanks for all of your help."

As I closed the front door behind me, I felt like a 300-pound weight had been lifted off my shoulders. I wanted to see Charlene more than I wanted to see my own father. I jogged the entire six minutes that it took me to get there. Charlene pulled up in a gray Mazda 626. It had tinted windows, so I didn't realize it was her until she rolled the window down.

"Hey, girl, get in," she said with that one of a kind smile.

"Charlene, I'm so sorry about the way I acted at the airport. I---"

"I know, don't worry about it," Charlene interrupted. "I am wondering what took you so long to call though. You had me worried sick about you."

"Well, why didn't you call me?"

"You were the one trippin in the airport. I figured if you wanted me, you would call."

"I understand. Can I have a kiss?"

"Yes you may," she said as she flung her hair out of her face and pressed her perfectly shaped lips against mine. "Now, how's that?" she said after we separated.

"I missed you so much the last two days. I was so confused."

"Confused about what?"

"Whether you and I could be an item or whether I was one of many. I almost didn't call because of that."

"Trust me, you can be my one and only if you wanna be."

"That makes me feel good to hear you say that. You are the one and only for me."

"You want to get a room and order room service?"

"That sounds real good to me," I replied. "Can I use your phone to call my mom and tell her not to wait up?"

"You don't ever have to ask to use my phone, you're my girl now and what's mine is yours, baby."

When we reached the hotel, I wanted to show Charlene that I was sincere. After getting out of the car, I walked around to the driver's side and reached my hand out for her. It felt strange at first, but I was going to get through this. As we checked in, an older dark complexioned middle-aged black man stared at us as he waited for Charlene's credit card approval. He was dressed in this tired looking black bus driver hat and a maroon uniform. The uniform had sparkling gold buttons down the center.

I hadn't felt this good in a long time. I was not going to give my new love any reason to believe that I was not totally into her. As she stood there getting the room key and getting instructions on how to get to our room, I pecked her on the lips. She was wearing a beige dress with a red flower print. She had on straw opened toed sandals and a straw hat. Her gold polished pedicure and manicure were immaculate. My body was trembling like a cold lawn mower engine. I yearned for her touch. How could a woman this beautiful be so in love with me? I fathomed. It didn't really matter, because I was crazy about her, and for now, she was my lady. I had made up my mind, if I felt as strongly in the morning about Charlene, I would tell my mother and father about her and our relationship.

"All set," the attendant said.

"You ready, baby?" Charlene asked.

"Yeah, let's go."

When we entered the elevator, I kissed her passionately. I felt like a high school girl in love for the first time. I wanted to tell her that I loved her, but I didn't want to sound too desperate. When we got to the room, I felt that it was definitely my turn to give not just receive. Tasting her wetness was a gripping, mouth-watering thought. As we opened the door to the bedroom, I felt that awesome throbbing feeling between my legs, again. After taking off my clothes, I helped Charlene take off her sexy white support bra. We kissed all the way to the shower. As we walked grudgingly to the bathroom, our feet slid ever so slowly across the dark brown carpet.

"I missed you Tanya."

"I missed you too," I replied while turning on the shower.

I grabbed a wash cloth and that small vanilla bar of hotel soap, and got in. I lathered up the cloth and began washing Charlene. I started at her shoulders and worked my way down. When I reached her breast, her nipples became erect. I couldn't help myself. I had to kiss them both. When I got to her midsection, I handed her the cloth. She handed the cloth back to me and told me to continue. She spread her legs and I began washing her. As I began to reach and pull, Charlene laid her head back and opened her mouth so that the water could flow through her mouth and down her body. The smooth feel of her vagina and crevice of her ass was invigorating. After washing her thighs, I got down on my knees so that I could wash her feet and in between her toes.

After washing her feet, I stood up. Because we were comparable in height, I could kiss her without bending down or looking up. She was perfect. My perfect lady. She took the cloth out of my hand, moved me to the back of the shower, and performed the same ritual on me. When she got to my breast she said, "You are my little Hershey's Kiss," as my dark nipples began to disappear in her mouth.

"And you are my Vanilla Shake," I muttered in her ear as I caressed her shoulders.

"I think I'm falling in love with you Tanya."

"I've all ready fallen in love with you," I replied.

"Oh, really?"

"Yes, really. I wanted to tell you earlier."

"I love you too my little Hershey's Kiss. Come on, lets get out and have some fun."

Charlene turned the water off and stepped out of the shower. Her hand found mine and she helped me out of the shower. We dried each other off with the large white hotel towels and walked hand in hand to the bed.

"This king-size bed is so huge that we could get lost," she said.

"I know what you mean," I mumbled. We got on the bed and held each other as we kissed as passionately as we did in the elevator. I was so into her that I was going to try everything I could possibly think of, leaving nothing to the imagination. I felt like, the kinkier the better. I began kissing her inner thighs before spreading her legs and devouring her beautiful pink mound. As I began licking her little man, she moaned, "Keep doing that, it feels so good." I continued. I was on my knees on the floor while she lay on the edge of the bed. I was enjoying her gorgeous pussy for only a few minutes before she asked me to get on the bed with her.

"I want to taste you while you taste me," she said.

I situated myself atop of her to complete the sixty-nine. My hands were planted firmly on the bed. As I enjoyed her, she enjoyed me. I had no idea how good another woman could taste. I pulled my elbows closer to my body revealing her beautiful booty. I licked her ass like I was enjoying a Popsicle.

"Hershey's Kiss, I didn't know you had it in you," she said.

"I didn't either, Vanilla Shake. You bring it out of me. You satisfy me and I want to satisfy you."

"Oh, you do Tanya, you really do. Just be your sexy chocolate self, and you will always please me. You wanna strap it on tonight?"

"Sure. I knew that I was going to have to learn sooner or later."

"Let me get it out of my purse," she said as she maneuvered her way around me. I enjoyed watching her ass shake as she retrieved the treat from her purse. "You have turned into a super-freak," Charlene said as she returned.

"Yeah, and I'm-loving-every-minute-of-it," I said. "Aren't you happy I'm letting it out on you?" I asked.

"Oh, you won't get any complaints out of me."

"All right then. Show me how to strap this thing on."

'It'll be my pleasure."

After strapping on the device Charlene asked, "Now how do you want me?"

"I want you on your back so that I can kiss you. I love kissing you. Maybe we can try doggy style later."

Charlene and I went at it all night. I did her, and she did me. I didn't realize how much fun this would be. I would have never guessed that the unforgettable night in the Airport hotel could get any better. I still couldn't say whether I would ever be attracted to another woman, or man for that matter. All I knew was that I loved Charlene with all of my heart.

***

On the day of Julian's trial, I was overjoyed when the judge read the verdict of not guilty. I guess Julian's faith in the Lord paid off. His lawyer was able to find the place that made the fake I.D. and Julian was free to go, Hallelujah! ...

CHAPTER 20

I tried the college thing and it just wasn't working out for me. My grades were atrocious and I was tired of being broke. I have always received compliments on my body, so I set out to become a stripper.

My first gig was in my hometown. I held a private show for one of my home girls who had been encouraging me to strip for years. Tammy Wilson was her name and she was really looking forward to my show. Needless-to-say- Tammy wanted to date me in high school, but seeing that she was not my type, I never gave her the time of day. Now that money was involved, she could set a date with me whenever she felt like it.

She invited five of her girlfriend over to her place, to watch me perform. I was a little nervous at first, but after the ladies started screaming and throwing money, I felt right at home. I must have racked in over three dollars in tips that night. My father and I had still not spoken in years, so I was staying with a high school classmate named, Alex .

On a cool morning, December 3, 2001, I secured the door to Alex's three-bedroom loft on the second floor of an unsettled house in Savannah, Georgia. I carried a black briefcase filled with my costumes down a flight of metal stairs and through a hallway to the front, where Alex's new red Chevrolet Corvette was parked in a space reserved for him. Alex was away on business and told me that I could use his car.

I stepped in behind the wheel, lit a Newport, and went through my mental checklist: three costumes, toiletries, and an address written on a sheet of paper for the house where I was to perform.

I wore black slacks, black Stacy Adams shoes, and a black rayon shirt. I looked at my gold watch and noticed that it was five minutes after nine. I had exactly fifty-five minutes to make it to my ten o'clock appointment. I started the car, backed out, changed gears, and moved expeditiously down the road under a brilliant sunny morning. Through the streets of Savannah I went, heading west on Abercorn Street for a few miles, then following highway 95 north as it shifted a little before intersecting with Highway 16.

With my back to the sun, I began the forty-five minute drive to Statesboro, Georgia. I liked this route of travel because State Troopers patrolled this highway infrequently and I knew I was going to have to hurry to make it to my appointment on time.

Turning up the volume on the radio, I listened to the tunes of Mary J. Blige's, "No More Drama." As I listened to the lyrics of the song, I reflected on my life. I thought back to my father's 21-year old dry cleaning business that was promised to me.

Now living the life of a stripper, I felt as though I hadn't lived up to any of my dreams or aspirations. I was making the quick money the best way I knew how. As Mary sang the words, "No more pain," I could only shake my head in disgust, as I continued to my destination. I wished for the hundredth time in my life that I had a family, maybe, to settle me down or perhaps to have someone to talk to around the house. Living the life of a stripper, had its moments, but it wasn't a life style that I would someday be proud of.

None of my family members knew of my occupation and I made sure I kept it that way. After passing the sign that read Pembroke, I knew that I was about 25 minutes from my destination.

When I entered Statesboro, banners that read "Georgia Southern Eagles 1-AA Football Champions," were everywhere. Georgia Southern, two days earlier, had beaten Florida A&M University by a score of 60-24 in the first round of the playoffs, and students were still in the streets partying two days later. *Boy they really take football seriously down here*, I thought to myself, as I continued at a snail's pace past the campus.

***

On my way to the house, however, I thought that I would be dancing for a room full of women. The deposit, for my appearance, was a hefty three hundred dollars.

There was only one woman, Ms. Rebecca Sims, who had booked me for herself. She was one of the ladies at my show in Savannah.

After the private show, Mrs. Sims paid me the remaining balance of two hundred dollars. "I hope that you won't say no, but will you sleep with me if I pay you an additional three hundred?"

What man wouldn't take a beautiful woman up on an offer like that? I reasoned. "Sure, why not," I replied.

Just as I got completely naked, I heard the front door, open. It was Mrs. Sims' husband. He was the owner of a construction company, and the project that he was working on, scheduled to end in a couple of more days, was completed ahead of schedule.

As Mr. Sims entered the bedroom, he saw me gathering my things and climbing out of the couples' bedroom window. Hastily, Mr. Sims located his pistol and began looking for bullets.

As he loaded his pistol, I scurried along to the car. Just as I got in and started the ignition, I heard a single gun shot blast. I didn't look back to see where he was aiming, I just put the car in gear, and sped off like a policeman on a high speed chase.

***

After nearly being shot, I planned a vacation to New York City. When I arrived in New York I took in a play and a movie early in the day. At night, I stopped by the diner that was next door to my hotel. I ordered a steak,

Caesar salad, and a bowl of chili. When I returned to my room, I decided to give my mother a call.

"William, I have some terrible news, son."

"What ?" I asked anticipating the worse.

"Your dad has suffered a stroke."

"Oh no," I said now crying.

"Where are you? I've called your apartment the past two days did you get my messages?"

"No, I didn't. I'm in New York on vacation. I'll be home as soon as I can, mom."

"Your father has been asking about you and says that he is ready to turn the business over to you now."

"Well, we will talk more in a couple of days. Tell dad I'll be there as soon as I can."

"Okay, sure thing," my mother added.

I decided to go back to the diner and grab something to eat while setting up my flight arrangement to go home. "Can I help you sir," the waitress asked.

"You sure can. Yesterday, I had the most delicious steak and chili I ever had. I would like to have another order of that if it's okay with you?"

"What would you care to drink with that?"

"Could you give me a minute?" I said after getting through to the airport on my cell phone. I learned that the flights were booked for the next couple of days, so I would have to spend at least three more days in New York.

After setting my flight arrangements, I looked up at the beautiful waitress who had returned and I asked, "How about a glass of Merlot?"

"One glass of Merlot coming up. Would you care for any dessert?"

"You are really on your job, young lady, suggestive selling and all. What is your name, if you don't mind me asking?"

"My name is Donna. Donna Short."

"Well you are very good at what you do, Ms. Short."

"Well, thank you. If you don't mind me asking, what do you do?"

"It's a long story, but I will be taking over my father's dry cleaning business very soon."

"I've never seen you around here before."

"I know. I'm not from around here. I live in Savannah, Georgia. I'm just here on vacation."

"How many more days will you be here?"

"Oh, I'll be here for a couple of more days. Why do you ask?"

"No reason, just wondered. I'll be back with your order in a minute," Donna said with a huge grin on her face.

When Donna returned with the food and Merlot, William stated, "You are a very pretty woman, are you married?"

"No, but I do have a three month old son."

"Do you have a boyfriend?"

"No. I was dating my son's father until I found out that he was married."

"Wow! Sorry to hear that. Well, I would like to go out with you while I'm here, if that's okay with you?"

"Um, I'll think about it."

"I'm staying at the hotel next door. I'm sorry. I didn't even tell you my name. I'm William. William Cole. How does tomorrow night at eight, sound?"

"I haven't told you I would, yet."

"I'm sorry. Excuse my rudeness."

Donna mulled it over for a couple of seconds. "Okay. I am off tomorrow night so tomorrow sounds perfect. Instead of giving you directions to my place, I'll just come over to the hotel tomorrow at eight. How's that?"

"Great! I'm staying in room 305. Call me when you get to the hotel, and I'll be right down."

She committed the number to memory. "I will. Would you like another glass of Merlot Mr. Cole?" Donna asked batting her eyes.

"No thank you. See you tomorrow."

***

To Donna's surprise, I had a romantic evening planned for her. She was promptly at the hotel at eight when the phone rang.

"Mr. Cole?" she asked.

"Please, call me William," I said. "I'll be right down."

When I got to the lobby, Donna was dressed in a pair of beige leather pants and a cream colored blouse. Her hair was tastefully done with Shirley Temple curls to accent her almond complexion. I asked her to go upstairs with me. At first she was hesitant, but then I assured her that I would be the perfect gentleman.

We took the elevator to the roof of the hotel. I had just, ten minutes earlier, laid out a blanket. On the blanket was a bowl of fruit, salad, blue cheese dressing, forks, knives, steak and potatoes. All of which was wrapped in aluminum foil. In an ice bowl was a bottle of Merlot and two wine glasses. I bought a small boom-box, and a Kenny G CD. The sounds of Kenny G were seductively filtering through the speakers.

"Mr. Cole I have never had an experience like this in my life. You really know how to treat a lady," Donna said melodramatically.

"I'm just happy that you like it," I said with a sly smile.

I spent the next two days with Donna and those were the best two days of my life. I learned about her family and heard a lot about her friends. I didn't want to leave, but I knew that my family needed me.

***

While on the plane headed to Atlanta and then Savannah, I thought about Donna the entire time. She was beautiful, thoughtful, and caring. I needed a family of my own and Donna's situation seemed too good to be true...

CHAPTER 21

Following college, I was offered a job as a copier salesperson. Charlene and I moved to Houston, Texas. Charlene was able to find a high school math teaching job with no problem. I was fairly successful, but wasn't happy with the sorry commissions Xerox was paying. I tried my hand at teaching, but after a few gun shots on school grounds, I decided to take the money that I had saved in preparation to move.

I was never satisfied working for someone else. I felt as if I were trapped into the vision of others instead of being myself. I seldom agreed with what my boss or principal thought were best practices for the organization, and was chastised for having different views and opinions. I knew I was smart and I knew that what I had to offer was valid and worth respecting. While working for someone else, I had to attend their stupid meetings and do exactly what they told me to do, even if I was certain that I had a better solution. I told my boss at Xerox that I could do a better job than he could at running the place, and of course, he showed me the door.

Now that I was fired, I had ample time to search the web for cities that were booming economically as well as accepting of my lifestyle. Texas wasn't too fond of lesbian relationships, so I knew I wanted to move elsewhere anyway. New York was the most accepting but I refused to live in the bitter cold again. Los Angeles was second in the acceptance category, followed by San Francisco and Atlanta. The cost of living was too high in California, so Charlene and I agreed on Atlanta.

***

After visiting a few banks, I got the money I needed to open my own business. I was able to secure speaking engagements at Clark Atlanta University, The University of Miami, Hampton University, Howard University, and Tennessee State University... just to name a few.

CHAPTER 22

When I reached Savannah and then the hospital, I was saddened to see my dad under these circumstances. My mom and sister Monique were there in tears. He was always so strong. How could this be happening to him?

"I had a stroke William, I'm not dead yet. Come on over here and give your old man a hug," my father said while raising his right arm slowly. That was when I noticed that the left side of his body was paralyzed.

"I'm so sorry, Daddy," I said as tears flowed freely from my eyes.

"Wipe your face son, we'll get through this. I knew that my health was fading several months ago. I have everything in place for you to take over the cleaners. Your mother and I have enough money to last us a lifetime so the money you make from the cleaners is all yours. Give your sister a little from time to time, would you son," Dad said as we all laughed.

"I will Dad," I said as I forced him a slight smile.

"So tell me son, do you have a girlfriend?"

"Kinda," I said excitingly. "I met a young lady when I was in New York and she is a great woman pops."

"Marriage material, son?" Dad asked.

"I think so. We have been talking virtually non-stop on the phone. I would love to fly back out there and spend more time with her."

"Well, I can start your pay this week and you can fly back there and spend a few weeks with her before you take over the store. How's that?"

"Thanks dad, that would be great," I said wiping a tear from my eye...

CHAPTER 23

After nearly a year and a half on the college circuit speaking, I thought that it was time to rest and to treat myself. I wasn't rich yet, but I was certainly on my way. After buying my mother a brand new house, I decided to invest in my first luxury car. I can remember when I went to purchase the car and how nerve racking that experience was. I purchased a black convertible Mercedes SL 500.

I walked into the dealership wearing a pair of old dingy blue jeans and a red sweatshirt. My dad was in town visiting, so I was riding around in his gray beat-up pick up truck. When I pulled up on the Mercedes lot in the pick-up, sales representatives avoided me like I had a "I'll work for food sign" affixed to my clothing. After several salesmen walked past me as though I was transparent, I demanded some attention.

Finally, a salesman approached me. The sales consultant looked at what I was wearing and what I was driving and immediately said rudely, "Yeah, what's up?"

"What's up? Is that how you greet customers here?" I asked.

"Oh, I didn't know that you were in the market for a car."

"Well I was, but you are awfully rude. Is there someone else I can speak to? I don't want to do business with you?"

"Yeah, sure. It's better that you waste someone else's time anyway."

I ran my hand on the back of my neck, where tension had began to gather. I didn't respond. I quietly waited for the next consultant. I heard a metallic click from an office door. When I looked up, I noticed a sales associate on his way over to me. I asked him how long he had been with the dealership. He told me that it was his second week and he was just starting to get a grasp of what he was supposed to be doing.

My dad taught me years ago that in the car business the term "citizen" means that the customer has excellent credit. Car salesmen ask you two qualifying questions; who financed your last car or how is your credit. If you tell them the name of a major bank or that you have excellent credit, they will assume that you are a citizen. I can recall my dad saying, "If you don't have excellent credit, it will be as if you are from a different country. You can't buy a damn thing."

"Well, seeing that you are new at this, can I give you a bit of advice?" I said to the salesman.

"Sure young lady, I'm all ears."

"I know your mother probably used to tell you, never judge a book by its cover. Am I right?"

"You sure are."

"Well that sales consultant over there, apparently felt as though he was wasting his time with me because I didn't look like I could buy a car. I want that $80,000 black convertible that's parked out front. Let me give you my information so that you can get paid. And oh by the way, I'm a citizen."

"A what?" he asked.

"Oh, never mind. Let's just fill out the application."

When I got home and parked in the garage, there was a note affixed to the door. The note read, "Take off your clothes as you're walking toward the bathroom."

I knew Charlene was up to something, so I played along. When I reached the bathroom, the lights were off and there were white floating candles burning in the tub. There was another note on the bathroom door. "Finish getting undressed, close your eyes and put your hands on your head." Again I played along. Just as I placed my hands on my head, I felt Charlene's lips against the small of my back. She stood up and whispered in my ear "I've got a surprise waiting for you in the bedroom, so don't be long," she said and walked away. I climbed in the tub, lathered up my rag and washed every inch of my body. I toweled off and headed to the room. When I opened the door to our bedroom I noticed that our bed was covered with white towels. *That's strange, I thought. Our bed is usually decorated with beautiful SILK SHEETS.* As my eyes racked across the room, I was stunned to see a man standing in the corner. Charlene introduced us and told me that he was a masseuse and it was time for me to be pampered.

I was certainly relieved to hear that because this man had seen me butt naked. He instructed me to lie across our bed and to relax. While I was enjoying my massage, Charlene was putting the final touches on dinner and setting the table. I had never had a massage and it felt weird at first, but eventually I loosened up and enjoyed it. After my massage I walked into the kitchen.

Charlene was wearing her white nylon see-through gown, with white panties and matching bra. She was looking as sexy as ever. I wanted to surprise her, but I didn't want her to be too surprised. She may have thought I bought the car for her, and I never want to disappoint my lady.

"Hey, Vanilla Shake."

"Hey baby. Did you enjoy your massage?" she asked before giving me a peck on the lips.

"It was wonderful," I responded. "I have something I want to show you."

"Oh you do, huh?"

"Yes. Come with me to the garage."

"Let me slip on my robe and slippers."

After making it outside, Charlene asked, "Is this ours?"

"Well, I actually bought it for you, but if you don't mind, I want to drive it most of the time," I said laughingly.

"Oh girl, stop tripping. You deserve it. My baby has been working her ass off. I'm happy that you finally bought yourself something nice. It's definitely you, black and sexy."

"Thanks, Vanilla Shake, I'm happy you like it."

"Oh I do. But it still doesn't stop me from wanting to have a refreshing dinner with my girl. So, come on in, let's eat. We can come back out later and take it for a spin."

"I'm right behind you."

"After dinner, you can take me for a ride."

"I drove home, so you can drive it tonight."

"Sounds good. As I drive, you can show me all of the features of that incredible piece of work."

"I can do that."

We enjoyed a delectable meal. Charlene's cooking reminded me so much of mom's. She prepared grilled lemon pepper salmon steaks, steamed vegetables in a savory rich butter sauce, and the fluffiest rice pilaf I ever had. To top it off, she made homemade croissants. She was definitely finding her way deeper in my heart. We ate, sipped on Chardonnay, and talked about the day's events. As she spoke, her calming voice and sexy light brown eyes hypnotized me under the flickering of the candle placed in the center of the table. The light breeze from the ceiling fan created a sensual ebb and flow of Sharon's hair. I thank God everyday for bringing her into my life. She was prettier now than the day I met her. After two and a half years, my heart still overflowed with joy for the love of my life.

We finished our meal and jumped in the car. Charlene didn't care that night. She jumped in the car in her nightgown and black bedroom shoes, and assured me that no one would notice her in the middle of the night. She drove. We joked. She drove. We joked some more. When I got home, the phone was ringing off the hook.

"Hello," I said out of breath.

"It's mom. Donna is getting married. She's getting married at her church this Saturday at three o'clock. On your birthday, how fitting. She says that she has been trying to call you for months. Seeing that I got a new job and the new house that you bought me, she didn't know how to contact us. Luckily, I ran into her at the store today."

"Tell Donna, I'll be there."

CHAPTER 24

The next day, Charlene and I boarded a plane to New York. As I returned to my mother's house, Donna was there waiting for me. Happy to see her, I hugged her neck.

"Who's the lucky man?" I asked.

"His name is William Cole. He has a dry cleaning business in Savannah."

"Just as I told you during my internship, Savannah is a beautiful town. You'll love it there."

"Well, God has truly blessed me with a wonderful man who is happy to be the stepfather to my son. The only unfortunate thing is that his father suffered a stroke a while back, so he won't be here for the wedding. His mother and sister Monique are scheduled to arrive early Saturday morning. I've only spoken to them on the phone, so I am excited about finally meeting them in person. Wherever we go, as long as I'm with him, I'll be very happy."

"That's great. I'm so happy for you," I said.

"There are several other out-of-town guests flying in today. Tonight we are going to have a dinner party at the clubhouse for all of you. William and the rest of the guests will be there."

"What do we wear?"

"Oh it's casual attire."

When we got to the club house later that evening, I could not believe that Donna knew so many people. There must have been four-hundred people there, many of whom I had never seen in my life.

"Donna, who are these people?" I asked.

"Tanya I couldn't tell you. Most of them are my distant relatives who only show up at weddings or funerals."

"I was going to ask if you were living a secret life or something, because I am your best friend and I have never seen most of these people," I said jokingly.

"I know what you mean. Hell, I don't know most of them myself. I just know that we are related somehow."

"I hear you."

"Where did Charlene go?" Donna asked

"I don't know. She was right behind me," I said.

"Well, now I don't see William. I wanted to introduce both of you to my fiancé. Let me find him, I'll be right back."

Donna went one way and I went the other. I must have covered the entire clubhouse three times with no sign of Charlene. Donna was gazing out the door and noticed William's car pull up under the streetlight. He got out and opened the passenger side door. Donna was stunned to see Charlene getting out of the car. The two stood there and talked.

"I thought your name was Jared?" Charlene asked.

"Jared is my middle name. My first name is William."

Charlene and William talked for a few more minutes before Charlene walked towards the clubhouse. Donna moved away from the door as though she hadn't seen a thing. Moments later, William appeared.

"There you are baby. I've been looking everywhere for you," Donna said trying to keep a straight face. "I want to introduce you to a few of my friends."

"All right baby," William responded as he was being led to Tanya who is now accompanied by Charlene.

"This is my best friend Tanya and my friend Charlene," Donna said.

"It's a pleasure to meet both of you ladies," William said.

Donna was livid! She did her best to hide it though. I asked what was wrong, but she shook her head as to say-nothing, but she didn't utter a sound.

"Excuse us. William I need to talk to you," Donna said as she walked out the front door.

"Yeah. What's up Donna?" William asked as he joined her outside.

"I don't know what the hell is going on but I saw Charlene getting out of your car."

"What are you talking about?" William asked.

"Don't play me. I saw her get out of your car. How do you know her?"

"It's a long story baby."

"Well you better make it short and sweet."

"When I was in college, my dad disowned me for a while. During that time I did whatever I had to, to make ends meet. I met Charlene at a night club in Atlanta. She and several of her lesbian friends paid me to have sex with them."

"Paid you?"

"Yes, they paid me either three or four hundred dollars every time I had sex with them."

"How many times did you have sex with Charlene?'

"Once."

"Yeah, right."

"I'm serious, just once. I hadn't seen her again until now. I didn't want her to tell you, that's why you saw me talking to her."

"What other secrets are you keeping from me?"

"That's the only one, I swear."

"I'm not sure that I want to marry you?"

"Donna, that was in my past. I have been true to you since the day I met you."

"I'm not so sure about that. I'll talk to you later. I need some time to think," Donna said as she walked through the clubhouse, out the door, and into her car.

I ran out to the car to talk to Donna but initially she said, "Not now, Tanya." Moments later she said, "Get in, we need to talk."

We drove about a mile down the road and pulled into an empty parking lot.

"Tanya, did you know that Charlene slept with my fiancé?" Donna asked just as we pulled into the lot.

"What!"

"Charlene and William slept together years ago. He said she was part of a lesbian group that paid men to have sex with them. Did you know that Charlene paid men to have sex with her?"

"No!"

"It's not like she has slept with your man, why do you sound so upset?"

"Because she's my lover, that's why."

"Your Lover! First William, now you. Why is it that the two people I care about the most in the world, wait until two days before my wedding to tell me some shit like this? I don't want a lesbian as my matron of honor and I sure as hell don't want some male prostitute for a husband, Donna said as she sped out of the parking lot, heading back to the party. "Get out of my car!" Donna yelled as she pulled up in front of the clubhouse.

When I went back inside, I found Charlene sitting next to the door. She had her head down as though she was depressed or in deep thought. I did not know about her paying men to have sex with her, especially now knowing that William was one of her clients. I was quite appalled.

I walked right up to Charlene and asked, "Why didn't you tell me that you used to pay men to have sex with you?"

"What?"

"You heard me!"

"You never asked," Charlene said and rolled her eyes. "Did you tell Donna or your folks about us?"

"That has nothing to do with it, but I've told Donna already and she is mad as hell with me. You're right, I haven't told my folks yet. Now, I'm not sure if I want to. I thought I knew you. I'm not sure that I'm ready to tell my mom anything."

"You know what? I'm going back to Atlanta. I don't need this shit. I've been good to you since the day we agreed to be lovers and you are bringing up old shit and you still haven't told your mother about us."

"You're right. I'm just confused right now. Please don't leave Charlene. I'll tell my mom, just not now. I will tell her after the wedding, I promise."

"That's not good enough. You told me a while back that you loved me and that you would never be ashamed of what we have. You lied to me. I'm catching the next flight out," Charlene said and walked out, slamming the door behind her.

I tried to stop her while she called for a cab from her cell phone. She shoved me to the side and kept walking. I had driven my mom's car that night so I walked out to the car, got in, and cried like a baby. In one hour, I had lost my best friend and my lover. As I drove home, I thought of the wonderful years of friendship that Donna and I shared. Donna was the one person that I could count on for anything. I kicked myself for not telling her about my relationship with Charlene earlier. Charlene and I have incredible chemistry, and I felt like I would die without her. Regardless of whether I would ever see

Charlene again, I was sure that this was unquestionably the right time to tell mom about the relationship that Charlene and I shared.

***

As I entered my mom's house she could see that I had been crying. "What's wrong," mom asked.

"I've got to tell you something that I have never told you before."

"Did someone die?"

"No mom, nothing like that. Charlene and I have been lovers for some time now."

"Lovers!"

"Yeah mom, lovers. She left me today because I hadn't told you about us."

"Who were all those guys you have been telling me about over the years?" Mom asked.

"There were no guys, just me and Charlene. I didn't know how you would react so that was why I kept saying 'he' when I should have been saying 'she'."

"With the hell that your dad put me through, I can't blame you for having a woman as your lover," mom said with laughter in her voice.

"I was afraid that you would disown me. I have heard you bad mouth lesbians before and I sure as hell didn't want you coming down on me. You used to talk so negatively about lesbians sometimes that if I—"

"I know baby, I know," mom interrupted. "I was talking about the two lesbians that I knew. I never said anything negative about their sexual orientation; it was the way that they carried themselves that I had a problem with."

"Well, I think I have lost Charlene forever."

"I'm sorry about that baby. Everything is going to be all right," mom said as she held me in a tight embrace.

Later that night I received a call from Donna apologizing to me and explaining that what happened in William's past should stay in the past. She went on to say that if William could accept her, and her illegitimate son as his own, and the three of them as his very own family, the least she could do is forgive him for his past.

***

On Donna's memorable wedding day, when the doors to the church opened, Donna stood motionless as the rest of us were in awe of how beautiful she was. Seconds later, her one of a kind smile, illuminated the entire church. As her father joined her, the congregation stood to its feet. When the pianist played the first note to "Here comes the bride" tears flooded my eyes. As she approached the altar, my smile widened. *Donna was a beautiful bride.*

Donna and William were married at exactly three o'clock. Following the wedding, the crowd dispersed on its way to the reception hall. Donna, William, and the rest of the wedding party, left the church to join the their guest at the reception.

***

When they arrived at the reception hall, hundreds of people were there waiting to party with them, me included. I was elated for Donna, but inside I was tattered. Knowing that any outward display of sadness would only spoil Donna's wedding day, I remained focused on the business at hand.

I truly wanted the love of my life to be with me enjoying this once in a lifetime endeavor. But she was hundreds of miles away. *I should have let the entire world know a long time ago, how much I love you Charlene Bedford.*

When Charlene left me, I realized that I had not only lost my lover, I had also lost my best friend. Just as I began to start feeling sorry-for-myself all over again, Mom appeared with Charlene.

"Charlene, I am so happy to see you," I said as I ran to her and started crying again.

"Your mom flew to Atlanta and told me everything."

"I'm sorry Charlene. I should have told everyone about us sooner."

"I accept your apology," Charlene said.

"I love you Charlene Bedford," I said.

And right there, in front of everyone, I kissed her.

Atlanta native **James D. Jackson** is also the author of *Wrong Perception, and Generations to Follow: How to Make Straight A's in School*. After being labeled as learning disabled during his childhood, he has worked tirelessly to overcome his disability. He has earned five college degrees to include a Ph.D., and he lectures extensively on a variety of topics. He lives in Savannah, Georgia.

To book Dr. Jackson for speaking engagements or to order additional copies of the book, call toll free: 1 (866) 849-4058 Or log onto www.regalpublishing.com